"Jed!" The word was a startled whisper.

"You ought to look where you're going, Caitlin." He glared at her, then turned away.

"Jed," she cried quietly. "Can't you even talk to me?"

"What is there to say?" he rasped.

"Anything," she pleaded. "You treat me as if you hardly even know me. You never told me why you walked out last year."

"You mean you haven't figured that out yet? Come on, Caitlin. You're not stupid."

"I was going to tell you everything."

"But you didn't." His voice was scathing. "You let Diana suffer for six months while you were out having a good time."

There were tears in Caitlin's blue eyes. "I've been trying to make up for that."

But could she ever completely make up for causing the horrible accident? Or was she too cowardly to try?

Other Bantam Starfire Books you will enjoy

EVVIE AT SIXTEEN by Susan Beth Pfeffer
FAMILY REUNION by Caroline B. Cooney
FORBIDDEN CITY by William Bell
HEARTBEAT by Norma Fox Mazer and Harry Mazer
NOT JUST PARTY GIRLS by Jeanne Betancourt
SOMEWHERE BETWEEN LIFE AND DEATH by Lurlene McDaniel
TELL US YOUR SECRET by Barbara Cohen
TIME TO LET GO by Lurlene McDaniel

Caitlin

TRUE LOVE

Created by
Francine Pascal

Written by
Joanna Campbell

BANTAM BOOKS
NEW YORK • TORONTO • LONDON • SYDNEY • AUCKLAND

The story and all characters are fictional and any resemblance to any persons, living or dead, is purely coincidental.

RL 7, age 12 and up

TRUE LOVE

A Bantam Book / January 1986
Produced by Cloverdale Press, Inc.
Conceived by Francine Pascal.

The Starfire logo is a registered trademark of Bantam Books, a division of Bantam Doubleday Dell Publishing Group, Inc. Registered in U.S. Patent and Trademark Office and elsewhere.

ISBN 0-553-25295-X

Published simultaneously in the United States and Canada

Bantam Books are published by Bantam Books, a division of Bantam Doubleday Dell Publishing Group, Inc. Its trademark, consisting of the words "Bantam Books" and the portrayal of a rooster, is Registered in U.S. Patent and Trademark Office and in other countries. Marca Registrada. Bantam Books, 666 Fifth Avenue, New York, New York 10103.

TRUE LOVE

1

Caitlin Ryan stopped dead in her tracks as she looked across the lawn of the Highgate campus and saw Jed Michaels walking toward the science building. She'd hoped and prayed not to see him on her first day back at school, but on a campus as small as Highgate Academy that was almost asking for a miracle.

Apparently he hadn't seen her. Nevertheless, she couldn't draw her eyes away from Jed's tall, athletic frame. She couldn't help noticing how the hot Montana sun had tanned his handsome face and lightened his thick, wavy brown hair over the summer.

Her heart lurched as she remembered their last night together. She hadn't seen him for three months, since the night he'd walked out on her at their prom, after telling her he never

1

wanted to see her again. His words had haunted her all summer as she tried to understand how he could have turned against her so suddenly.

"Caitlin, are you all right? You look as if you've seen a ghost."

Quickly Caitlin pulled herself together and smiled brightly at the good-looking, dark-haired boy standing at her side. "Don't be silly, Laurence. Didn't your mother ever tell you there're no such things as ghosts?"

Laurence Baxter's smile brought dimples to his cheeks. "Well, in that case," he said, "I'm glad I'm wrong. It's just that you looked so white a moment ago."

"It must have been the heat." Even though Caitlin was five foot eight, she had to lean her head back a little to look up at Laurence's face. He was so sweet, she thought to herself, and he'd really been her salvation since they'd started dating during the summer. He knew all about her and Jed, yet he still wanted her. Caitlin knew how lucky she was to have Laurence in her life. She linked her arm through his and forced all signs of pain from her perfect features.

"It's kind of exciting being back," he said, glancing around the beautiful Highgate grounds.

"You sound just like Ginny," Caitlin noted. "Have you two been comparing notes?"

"I haven't seen her yet," he said. "How is she?"

"She had a good summer," Caitlin said. "In fact, we stayed up half the night talking. That's why I missed breakfast."

"Great way to start off the year," Laurence said teasingly.

Caitlin laughed. "Knowing the cafeteria food, I don't think I missed much."

"*Au contraire, mon amour,*" Laurence said. "We had eggs Benedict and homemade blueberry muffins this morning. Delicious." He smacked his lips.

"Well, I'm on a diet anyway," Caitlin said, patting her flat stomach.

Arm in arm they continued walking over the brick walk toward the main classroom buildings. Suddenly three girls ran toward them. Caitlin had been so busy the night before, first unpacking, then talking to her roommate Ginny, she hadn't had a chance to see her old friends.

"Caitlin!" one of the girls shrieked. "How *are* you?"

"Hey, Morgan," Caitlin answered. She grinned at Morgan as Gloria gave her a quick hug. "How was your summer?"

"Incredible," said Morgan. "Maine was terrific, and I met the most *interesting* guy!"

"Oh, really? What about Roger?"

"You don't have to mention anything about i to Roger." Morgan winked.

"Hi, Jessica," Caitlin cried. "God, Gloria, look at your tan!"

"Not bad, eh?" Gloria agreed. "You're looking good yourself."

"Thanks. Hey, no one's said hi to Laurence."

"Hi to Laurence," Morgan said, giggling.

Jessica asked Laurence how his summer had been, and Morgan used the opportunity to lean close to Caitlin and whisper, "What happened to Jed?"

"I'll talk to you later," Caitlin whispered back, the smile never leaving her lips. "So where are you all off to?"

"Another year of drudgery," Gloria quipped.

"Well, Laurence and I are on our way to English lit. Walk along with us if you want," Caitlin offered.

The girls followed Caitlin along the brick path that led to the academic buildings.

"Did you hear that Kim Verdi and Jim broke up over the summer?" Gloria asked.

"No, I hadn't," Caitlin answered, her stomach twisting at the mention of the words "broke up."

"I just talked to Kim. She's taking it pretty

4

hard. Jim started dating another girl during his vacation on Cape Cod."

"Well, Kim always took him for granted, anyway," Morgan interrupted. "Did you see the car Matt was driving?"

"No, what is it?"

"A classic Corvette!" Morgan exclaimed.

"You're kidding. I've got to check it out." Gloria grinned wickedly.

"The car or Matt?" Jessica teased.

They'd reached the steps of the building where Caitlin and Laurence had English. "There's not enough time to catch up on everything. We've got to get together tonight!" Morgan exclaimed. "Shall we meet in your room as usual, Caitlin?"

"Laurence and I are going out tonight," Caitlin answered, hiding the relief she felt. She didn't particularly want to get together with the old group. They'd want to know what happened between her and Jed, and she wasn't ready to talk about it.

"We can do it tomorrow night instead, Caitlin," Laurence offered.

"No, Laurence," she said. Turning to her friends, she added, "I know you'll understand. We'd planned to go riding together, and I'm really looking forward to it."

Laurence's delight was obvious. His warm

brown eyes smiled down at her. "Sure, if you'd rather." He reached over and squeezed her hand.

"Let's make it another night, okay?" Caitlin said gaily to the girls. "There'll be plenty of time."

"Yeah, I guess," Morgan mumbled disappointedly. Both she and Gloria thrived on gossip.

"We'd better get going, Laurence, or we'll be late for class. See you later," Caitlin called to the others as she led Laurence into the building and down the corridor to their classroom. "That Morgan never changes," she added quietly to him.

He laughed. "I'm glad you're not like her."

Caitlin sighed. There was a time, not too long ago, when she *was* as catty and self-centered as Morgan. But that was before the terrible, tragic events of the past year. As rough as it had been for her, she had to admit that the experience had made her more aware of those faults, and she'd worked hard at becoming a more caring and sensitive person. She was glad that she hadn't gotten to know Laurence well until the past summer. He never would have liked the old Caitlin, and she didn't know how she could have survived the past few weeks without him.

But her brief glimpse of Jed had unnerved her.

She didn't know how she'd deal with having to face him every day. Nor did she know what she'd do if his anger at her led him to reveal the awful secret he'd discovered, the secret that had turned him so completely and irrevocably against her.

Late that afternoon Caitlin hurried up the dorm stairs to the room she shared with Ginny Brookes. Ginny had been Caitlin's roommate and best friend since they'd entered Highgate in their freshman year. Ginny was also one of only three people on campus who knew that Jed had broken up with Caitlin, although even she didn't know why. Jed's cousin, Emily Michaels, and Laurence were the others.

"Hi, there!" Ginny called as Caitlin burst into the room. Her smile quickly turned into a frown as she regarded Caitlin. "You look upset."

"No, no," Caitlin said, protesting, but now that she was in the privacy of her room, she relaxed her artificial pose. She sighed. "I should know better than to try to hide the truth from you. I saw Jed this morning."

Ginny looked at Caitlin with sympathy. "It's going to be rough. You're not going to be able to avoid him all year, you know."

"I know."

"Did you talk to him?"

"No, I only saw him from a distance. I don't think he saw me." Slumping down on her bed, she sighed again. "That was bad enough, but everywhere I went today everyone kept asking me, 'How's Jed?'"

"It's understandable. You two were inseparable last year." Ginny fiddled with her pencil as she added, "You sure you don't want to tell me what happened? I mean, it was strange. One minute you were king and queen at the prom; the next minute he dumped you."

"I—I can't, Ginny," Caitlin said. She couldn't tell her best friend why Jed had walked out without revealing the secret she'd kept from everyone at Highgate—that *she* was the one who was responsible for the accident that had crippled Dean Foster's son, Ian, the year before. Jed left her because he'd discovered the awful truth. Now he hated her for having kept silent and for letting another girl, Diana Chasen, take the blame. "Maybe someday, I can. But not now," she added.

"I'm always here if you need me," Ginny said. "But you're going to have to think up something to tell everyone else."

"I'll just tell them we had a big argument and broke up. It happens all the time, right?" Caitlin said dispiritedly. "Besides, it's not that far from the truth. Jed made it pretty clear in his letters to

Emily that he didn't want to have anything to do with me anymore."

"And all this time I thought he was a guy with great taste," Ginny said. "At least Laurence had the good sense to grab you while he could."

"Thanks." Caitlin kicked off her white sandals. "Ginny, there's something I've got to tell you," she announced.

"Go ahead," Ginny said, sitting up straight in her desk chair.

"I didn't tell you everything I did this summer. You know I told you I did some volunteer work at the hospital?"

"Yeah?"

"Well, I went because Diana Chasen was there. I wanted to try to help her."

"You're kidding! Why? You were never friends with her."

"I felt sorry for her. After Jed left me, I felt so bad that I wanted to do something good for someone. And after working with Ian all last spring, I felt closer to Diana. I wanted to see her get better." Caitlin still couldn't bring herself to tell Ginny that she'd been motivated by guilt to help Diana, who, in the aftermath of the tragic accident, had been forced to leave Highgate. She'd then suffered a nervous breakdown and was hospitalized with anorexia nervosa.

"So what happened?"

"It took a long time, but she recovered from

the anorexia. Now she's enrolled in a school in Pennsylvania. I think she's going to be all right."

"Well, I'm glad to hear that. The rest of you never thought much of Diana, but I thought she was a sweet kid."

"She is. Now that I've gotten to know her, I really like her. We've become pretty good friends."

"Does Jed know this?"

Caitlin nodded. "But it doesn't make any difference. I didn't hear from him all summer."

"I'm sorry, Caitlin. It just doesn't make any sense to me."

Shrugging, Caitlin sighed. "All he said that night was something about my using people, and then he walked away." Caitlin didn't want to tell Ginny how coldly he'd spoken or how close he'd come to using her body to express his anger. Jed had turned into a different person that night, and Caitlin wanted to erase the entire scene from her memory.

"Hmm," Ginny mused. "I could have understood his saying that in the beginning of the year, but you really stuck with him. You were good to him."

"I've just got to get him out of my mind now," Caitlin said. "All of that's in the past."

"Are you going to keep working with Ian this year?"

Caitlin nodded. "I wrote to him over the summer. He was homesick away at that school. It was especially hard on him having to celebrate his birthday there, so his parents thought he might make more progress back here at Highgate."

"I'm not surprised he got homesick. He's only a little boy." Ginny untangled her long legs from her chair and got up from the desk. "I'm supposed to meet Bert at the stables in a little while, but I'll stay here if you want. Did you want to talk some more?"

"No, I guess not."

"Chin up, kid," Ginny said. "It's only the first day of school. You and Jed may work it out yet."

Caitlin shook her head. "I don't think we'll ever work it out."

"Why don't you come down to the stables with us, so you don't have to sit here and mope?"

"I'm not moping," Caitlin insisted. "Besides, Laurence and I are riding after dinner. I think I'll start organizing my books now."

"Okay. I'll see you later."

"Yeah." But as Ginny left the room, Caitlin dropped her chin onto her palms and sighed. It was only her first day back at Highgate, and already she realized the pain of losing Jed wasn't going to go away easily. How, she wondered, was she going to survive an entire year with him so close—yet so unattainable?

11

2

"What a gorgeous sunset!" Caitlin cried, looking out across the jump courses and sweeping meadows toward the pink-and-orange clouds over the western hills.

"This is a nice time to ride," Laurence said as he stopped his horse beside her. "Wish I'd had Satellite here last year."

Caitlin gave her own horse's neck a pat. "Duster would miss me if he weren't here. Wouldn't you, boy?" As if understanding her, the horse nickered.

"I meant to tell you," Laurence said thoughtfully. "Some of the guys were talking today about this year's fund-raiser and wondering if someone could come up with an idea to top last year's."

"Oh, really? When was this?"

12

"At lunch. I heard Roger Wake and Tim Collins joking around."

"I'm glad it's not my problem this year," Caitlin said. "I had my hands full with last year's fund-raiser, and that was enough for me."

"Hmm, that's too bad. Roger was thinking of asking you to come up with another idea like your male beauty contest."

"It's up to him this year. He's the new student council president."

"Only because you decided not to run last spring."

Caitlin shrugged. "I figured I'd be pretty busy this year."

"Busier than you thought, if I have anything to say about it," Laurence said. He was silent for a minute, then said, "Maybe I shouldn't mention this, but I saw Jed today."

Caitlin winced, and Laurence noticed.

"Sorry. I knew I should have kept my big mouth shut."

"No." She forced her voice to sound light, as if it didn't matter. "That's all right. You're my boyfriend now, remember? You and I get along much better than Jed and I ever did." She didn't dare look at Laurence for fear he'd see the lie in her blue eyes. Quickly she changed the subject. "I got a letter from Diana today. She sounds as if she really likes her new school."

Laurence smiled. "I'm happy for her."

"Me, too. She invited us to come up over Thanksgiving break, but I'm sure my grandmother will already have made plans."

"We'll work something out. Your grandmother doesn't know how much you did for Diana, does she?"

"Not really. She didn't approve of my volunteering, so I never talked to her much about it."

Caitlin didn't add that she rarely talked to her grandmother about anything that was important to her. She didn't see why she should; Regina Ryan had rarely been affectionate to her. Oh, she'd given Caitlin everything money could buy—the best designer clothes, vacations in Europe, boarding school, her own horse, and the luxury of her home, Ryan Acres. But Caitlin had always felt her grandmother only cared for her and raised her because she'd *had* to. Caitlin's mother, Regina's daughter, had died in childbirth.

Regina Ryan had never told Caitlin who her father was. She had said only that he had deserted her after she was born. Caitlin hadn't known his identity until she met him accidentally over the summer at the hospital where she'd volunteered to help Diana. He was Dr. Gordon Westlake, the hospital's administrator. He claimed he'd never known her mother was pregnant, that Regina Ryan had whisked her daughter away before he'd been able to marry her. Caitlin was sure he was lying, and so she had rejected him, just as she believed he'd rejected her as an infant.

Caitlin was thankful that Laurence was looking off at the beautiful Virginia landscape and didn't notice how she was scowling. She swallowed and said brightly, "I'm going over in the morning to see Ian."

He turned his head to look at her. "The Fosters will like that."

"In their last letter this summer, they told me how much he'd missed me."

"You still haven't told them the truth, have you?" Laurence asked quietly.

Caitlin dropped her eyes, then looked over at him sadly. "I was going to. I told Diana I wouldn't feel right unless I did, but she didn't want me to. She said she was making a new life for herself and didn't want me upsetting the Fosters even more."

"But it bothers you," Laurence stated.

"Yes." She sighed and gave him another sad look, which immediately touched his heart.

He reached over and squeezed her hand, the one that held the reins. "You've done everything you could," he said sympathetically.

Caitlin gave him a weak smile. "We'd better get back before it gets dark."

"Right. Race you to the end of the pasture!"

"You're on!" Caitlin suddenly gave him a broad smile and heeled Duster. Then they were off, with Caitlin gaining a length's lead before Laurence got Satellite up to speed. Clumps of grass flew out from behind their mounts' hooves as they galloped across the meadow toward the gate leading back to the Highgate stables. Caitlin was laughing when she pulled Duster up at the fence and turned to see Laurence pounding up a moment later.

"You cheated," he called, grinning.

"Duster's just fast off the line."

"Next time, let's do some fences, too."

"Okay. Thursday night?"

"It's a date."

Even as she smiled up at Laurence, Caitlin was thinking not of Thursday night, but of Jed. She could never love Laurence the way she'd loved Jed. Laurence was sweet, dependable, and steady. If she'd never met Jed, she could have very easily fallen in love with Laurence. But Caitlin knew she'd never feel more than a deep friendship and appreciation for him. Her heart was still committed to Jed, the boy who'd made her heart sing in a way she'd never thought was possible.

Yet none of that mattered anymore. Jed no longer loved her.

Caitlin set her alarm for six-thirty the next morning so she could get to the Fosters' at least fifteen minutes before her first class at eight-thirty. She wondered what it would be like to see Ian again. Would he be glad to see her after three months? That was a long time in a little boy's life. They'd spent so much time together the spring before, trying to strengthen the muscles in his legs. It had eased her guilt to be able to work with him. So many times she'd come close to telling his parents that it was she, not Diana, who was responsible for his condition. Yet Caitlin couldn't bring herself to confess that she'd accidently left the garden shed door unlocked, which had enabled Ian to get in and swallow some poisonous chemicals stored there. If she told them the truth, she was certain they'd hate her, and now that she'd grown close to them, she wouldn't have been able to stand that. And Diana's telling her that she didn't mind if the Fosters still blamed her had made it easier for Caitlin to continue living the lie.

Caitlin arrived at the Fosters' house, one of the elegant brick faculty houses on campus, just as Dean Foster was leaving for his office.

"Caitlin." Dean Foster was obviously delighted to see her. "I'm glad you've come. Ian asks about you all the time. Those thoughtful letters you wrote him over the summer really cheered him up."

"Oh, I wanted to write, Dean Foster. Ian's very special to me."

"Go on in. Elaine's giving him his breakfast."

Caitlin stepped through the front door and walked down the hall toward the kitchen.

She paused in the doorway and peeped through. Ian, in his wheelchair, had his back to her. His mother was placing a glass of milk on the tray, which was spread over the wheelchair arms.

Mrs. Foster saw Caitlin first and nodded slightly. Caitlin put a finger to her lips and tiptoed into the kitchen. Then she came around Ian's wheelchair and stopped in front of him, her broadest smile on her face. "Surprise!" she shouted.

The blond, curly-haired little boy nearly dropped his glass of milk. "Caitlin!" he cried. "Caitlin, you've come back!"

She stepped forward, took the glass of milk from his hand, then hugged him. "Oh, it's so good to see you! You're getting so big."

"I missed you, Caitlin."

"I missed you, too, but it was important for you to go to school this summer."

"I didn't like it. I liked the way you helped me better."

Caitlin felt like crying for the misery she'd caused this boy, but she blinked her eyes to force away the tears. "I want to help you again, Ian, if you'd like." She felt his strong little arms around her neck, and pressed her own arms tighter around him. She pulled back and looked down into his big blue eyes. "Why didn't you like school, Ian?"

"They made me do all these things I didn't like. And the teachers weren't fun, like you are. They didn't play animal games. They just made me do these yucky exercises that hurt my legs."

"We'll find fun things to do this fall, Ian," Caitlin assured him.

"I want to go on a treasure hunt."

"We can do that."

He grinned. "Can you come tomorrow after I go to school, Caitlin?"

"I'll be here," she promised.

With Caitlin's assurance that she'd be back, Ian turned to his mother. "Mom, I'm hungry. Can I have breakfast now?"

"You sure can," Elaine Foster said.

"I'll see you tomorrow, Ian. I've got to get to

class now. I'll come after school tomorrow so I can spend a longer time with you."

"Okay, Caitlin."

As Caitlin walked toward the hallway, Elaine Foster followed her and spoke quietly so Ian couldn't hear her. "I'm glad you came. He really missed you."

"I missed him, too. I was hoping to see him out of that wheelchair."

Mrs. Foster sighed. "The doctors told us there's been a lot of muscle regeneration. There's no physical reason why Ian can't walk—except that he won't try." Tears came to the older woman's eyes. "I've tried so hard with him, but I'm his mother. I'm soft. When he says no, I don't pursue it. You're so good because you're not easy on him, and he trusts you."

"I'll try to push him, Mrs. Foster."

"The doctors told us he's afraid of the pain. Once it begins to hurt, he stops trying."

Caitlin nodded. "I think I know how to help him forget the pain. I'll try."

Elaine Foster took Caitlin's hands. "We'd love to have you. Caitlin, I hate to take up so much of your time. Your grandmother was so concerned last spring about the strain on your schedule—"

"It's no strain," Caitlin cut in. "I like working with Ian. I'll be here tomorrow after class."

"I'll look forward to it. And, Caitlin, I'd like to pay you."

Caitlin quickly shook her head. "Thanks, Mrs. Foster, but I don't want any money. Helping Ian is something I want to do. See you tomorrow," Caitlin said before hurrying from the house.

Oh, Mrs. Foster, you've got it all wrong, she thought ruefully as she headed for her class. *If you knew the truth, you wouldn't even let me into your house much less make me such a generous offer. I should be paying you for all the pain and heartbreak I've caused.*

3

"Hi, everyone," Ginny said as she put her tray down in front of her regular chair in the cafeteria. Caitlin, Morgan, and Gloria were already seated around the table Caitlin had selected in her sophomore year as hers. Directly in front of one of the tall side windows, it had a view of Highgate's grounds and from it the girls could see the entire mahogany-paneled room that was unchanged from the days when it was the elegant dining room of a plantation manor house.

"Hi, Ginny," Morgan said absently as she nudged Caitlin's elbow. "My God, do you see Roger over there, talking to Jane Winthrop? I don't believe it!"

"I wouldn't worry about it, Morgan," Caitlin

said nonchalantly. "He's only flirting. Besides, what about that guy you met over the summer?"

"I'll see him over Christmas, if I'm lucky, and Roger is here now. What's he doing with *her*? She's only a sophomore." Morgan took a breath as she and the rest of the girls watched the redhead take Roger's arm and lead him to a table.

"Looks like you'd better do some homework, Morgan," Gloria warned.

"Don't worry," Morgan responded. "He has a date with me tomorrow."

Just then Jed Michaels carried his tray into the dining room.

Gloria looked in his direction and sighed. "Boy, is he gorgeous."

Caitlin forced her lips together and said nothing, but her eyes followed every move Jed made. He took a seat at the far end of the room, across from a cute, curly-headed blond. The brightness of her luminous green eyes was visible even at that distance.

"Who's he sitting with?" Ginny asked.

"Tara Langden," Morgan answered. "She transferred here this year from England. I heard that her father's connected with the British embassy in Washington. She's cute, isn't she?" Morgan glanced at Caitlin.

Caitlin said nothing, her face expressionless.

She'd already heard about the new girl on campus, but she wasn't about to let any of the others at the table know what she was feeling at that moment.

Again Morgan nudged Caitlin. "You still haven't told me what happened with you and Jed."

"Nothing."

"That's no answer. Right up to the night of the prom you and Jed were *always* together."

"That was last year. I have better things to do this year."

"Laurence?" Gloria asked.

"Exactly," she answered.

"Humph. They're hardly in the same league," Morgan said.

"How would you know?" Caitlin countered.

"I've got two eyes," Morgan said and snickered.

"And a big mouth," Gloria added.

Caitlin was studying Jed and Tara at the other side of the dining room. He didn't seem that interested in her—at least not so interested as she appeared to be in him. When he turned to say something to her, she smiled. Caitlin felt a sharp pang of jealousy.

"You know," Morgan said almost in a whisper to Caitlin, "Jed won't talk either. When I saw Roger last night, he said that Jed just clammed up about you. He told all the guys to mind their own business."

"You should follow his advice," Caitlin said shortly. "It's nobody's business but ours."

"But I'm your friend," Morgan persisted.

"Maybe when I talk to Roger, I should tell him about the guy in Maine," Caitlin said innocently.

"You wouldn't!" Morgan nearly dropped her sandwich.

"Then let up on Jed and me."

"I wasn't trying to pry," Morgan said as contritely as someone with her cunning could.

Caitlin glanced cautiously toward the other table. Jed had finished his lunch and was standing, getting ready to leave. Tara was still eating, and that made Caitlin feel better.

"Hey, can't you guys find something else to talk about?" Ginny asked, knowing how much Caitlin didn't want to be reminded about Jed.

"But what else is there but boys?" Morgan said with mock innocence. "Unless you want to tell us all about Cinnamon's latest exploits." She laughed. "There *is* more to life than horses," she added bitingly.

"Cut it out," Caitlin snapped, aware that Morgan had hit on a touchy subject with Ginny.

"Sorry." Morgan smiled sweetly. "I didn't mean to offend you, Ginny."

"That's better," Gloria said. "I think we're all

letting the pressures of senior year get to us. We need to cool out—have a party or something. What do you think, Caitlin?"

"Why are you asking me?"

"Because you're the best party planner this school's got. What do you say?" Gloria asked, prodding her.

Caitlin was about to bow out, saying she was definitely not in a party mood. But she stopped herself when she realized that a party might be just what she needed to help occupy her mind and keep her from dwelling on Jed. "That's a great idea, Gloria."

"When should we have it?" Gloria asked.

"As soon as possible. And let's do something different. Let's have the party outside, on the quad." The brick-paved quad separated the four main academic buildings at Highgate. "We can put up lights and hook up some stereos. It'll be great! I'll talk to Dean Foster about it," she added with rising enthusiasm.

Ginny beamed. "The old Caitlin has returned," she whispered so low that only Caitlin could hear her.

"Do you think the dean will let us do it?" Morgan asked with a frown.

"Why not? We're always having dances in the gym, and if we clean up afterward, what could be the problem? I'll ask him today before I go over to help Ian." She picked up her tray. "I've got to go. Meeting tonight, my room?" she asked.

"We'll be there," Gloria answered.

Caitlin's session with Ian that afternoon went better than she'd expected, thanks to a game she'd devised for him. She'd taken a big piece of construction paper, plotted out the perimeter of a castle, and molded some knights and horses and other game pieces out of clay. Ian had to get all the pieces into the castle in order to get to the hidden treasure, but he couldn't make any moves until he did his exercises, and the number of moves he made depended on how much effort he'd put in. Caitlin had noted that he endured the painful stretching of his muscles much more readily when the prospect of getting through the castle gate was in sight.

Laurence met her at the Fosters' at five to walk her back to the dorm, and she excitedly told him about her party plans, which the dean had approved.

"If you want some help setting up," Laurence offered, "I'm sure I can get a bunch of the guys together."

"That'd be great." She smiled up at him. "We'll need to move some of the chairs out of the gym and set up the stereo speakers. Do you mind?"

"Why should I mind?" He pulled his arm a little tighter around her waist, and his eyes told her he'd move mountains for her if he could.

Caitlin laughed to break the seriousness of the moment. "Some of the girls are getting together tonight in my room to make plans. I'll let you know all the details tomorrow."

"Weren't we supposed to go riding tonight?"

Caitlin gasped. "Tonight? Oh, Laurence, I thought it was tomorrow. I'm sorry," she said with dismay. "Could we make it then instead?"

"Sure. No problem. Maybe I had the wrong day myself."

As they reached her dorm, he paused on the brick path and turned to her. He touched her chin with his fingers. "Wish I could give you a kiss good-bye."

She looked around at the handful of students nearby. "Not here!"

He grinned. "I know. I'll see you at breakfast in the morning."

She nodded.

"Have a good meeting."

"We will."

The meeting did go well. Morgan, Jessica, and Gloria arrived exactly at seven and pulled the overstuffed pillows from Caitlin's bed to sit on.

Ginny was already sitting on her own bed, and Emily Michaels, whom Caitlin also had asked to come, arrived a few minutes later.

After some minor arguing, they agreed on the following Friday night for their party. Invitation would be by word-of-mouth, but since, between them all, they knew just about everyone on campus, there was little chance of anyone being excluded.

Their plans made, the conversation degenerated into a gossip session. Ginny stood up.

"I don't know about you guys, but I've got a busy day tomorrow. I'm going to take a shower."

"I guess we'd better get going, too," Jessica agreed. "Gloria, Morgan, you ready?"

Gloria stretched and yawned. "Sure. I've got to finish up a history assignment, anyway. See you tomorrow, Caitlin."

Within minutes the room was empty except for Caitlin and Emily, Ginny having gone to take a shower. Caitlin didn't mind Emily's staying—in fact, she welcomed the chance to spend some time alone with her. Emily was Jed's cousin, and Caitlin hoped the girl might have further insight as to how he was feeling about her at that point.

"I've hardly had a chance to talk to you since school started," Emily said sincerely. "How's it going?"

Caitlin shrugged. "Okay, I guess."

"But not great," Emily added perceptively. She and Caitlin had gotten to be good friends the year before when Jed and Caitlin had been dating. "Have you talked to Jed?"

"No. Have you?"

"A little, though he hasn't said anything about you two breaking up. It's the same as it was in his letters over the summer—he never mentions you."

"I was afraid of that," Caitlin said sadly. "I've seen him on my way to class and in the cafeteria, but he doesn't say hello or anything. He just looks the other way. Today I saw him having lunch with Tara Langden." Caitlin intended the comment as a lead-in for any news Emily might have, but Emily seemed surprised.

"Really? I met her the other day, but I wouldn't think she'd be Jed's type. She's a little on the dumb side, if you ask me. I haven't seen him with anyone in particular, although I've noticed a lot of girls looking at him." She paused, then looked over to Caitlin. "I don't mean to get your hopes up, but I think he's still in love with you."

Caitlin shook her head and sighed. "He has a strange way of showing it."

"Give him time. Maybe he's not sure what he wants." Again she paused. "You've been seeing a lot of Laurence."

"I'm so glad we got to know each other better this summer. I don't know what I would have done without him. He's so sweet. . . ."

"But he's not Jed."

Caitlin looked at her friend quickly, then said honestly, "No, he's not Jed."

"Listen," Emily said sympathetically, "I'll let you know if Jed says anything to me. Something tells me you two are going to work this out."

But instead of cheering her up, Emily's words made Caitlin even more depressed. The last thing she needed was false hope. No, she thought resolutely, she had to concentrate on building her relationship with Laurence. For all intents and purposes, Jed Michaels was dead to her.

4

"Looks as if the party's going to be a success," Laurence said cheerfully as he and Caitlin walked together across the lawn the next Friday night. The quad was already filled as they approached, and they could hear bursts of laughter and talk over the loud music that blared from the four huge speakers the boys had set up.

"It sure does," Caitlin agreed, despite the nervous quivers in her stomach. Organizing the party had kept her busy all week, but she was beginning to wonder at her wisdom in arranging it. It was likely Jed would be there, and the thought of seeing him and watching him flirt with other girls upset her. So far Caitlin had managed to avoid all the places where she'd be likely to see him, such as the soccer field. But she knew her luck was about to run out, and despite her resolve to forget him, she was afraid to test her feelings.

She and Laurence had gone riding nearly every night that week. The evening twilights were still long, and they'd been able to get in hour-long rides, practicing their jumping over the fences set up behind the Highgate stables. But as much as Caitlin enjoyed Laurence's company, she couldn't ignore the dull ache she felt when she remembered the hours she and Jed had spent coaching each other on the minor points of horsemanship. Why couldn't he forgive her? Why couldn't he love her again?

The questions gnawed at Caitlin. But she had to pretend she'd gotten Jed out of her system. She wanted everyone to think she was having a wonderful time, even though she felt like crying.

"You're awfully quiet," Laurence spoke up, interrupting her thoughts. "Is something wrong?"

She forced herself to concentrate on Laurence. "No, of course not. I was just wondering if I'd done everything I was supposed to. Do you think Roger and Tim remembered to pick up the soda?"

"It's all there. I knew you'd be concerned, so I checked before I came over to get you."

"Good, and I know Gloria and Jessica got the chips and stuff from the cafeteria staff. It's a good thing we had money left over in the student council treasury."

When they were a few yards away from the quad, Morgan broke away from a group standing under one of the trees and jogged over to them. "There you are! I thought you'd never get here."

"I wanted to take a shower and change," Caitlin explained, although, in fact, she'd taken her time getting dressed, not wanting to arrive at the party before there was a crowd gathered.

"I like that outfit." With cool appraisal, Morgan scanned the white, full-sleeved jump suit that looked so chic on Caitlin's tall, well-proportioned figure. "Where'd you get it?"

"Georgetown." Even though Caitlin was surprised at the compliment from the usually catty Morgan, she smiled and said, "Thanks, Morgan. You look nice yourself."

Morgan fussed with the sleeves of the over-sized, multicolored shirt she wore over cropped pants. "Thanks," she said as if expecting the nod of approval. "It's an original Mugler. Mother got it for me on her last trip to Paris."

Caitlin had already turned her gaze away from Morgan, toward the crowd.

"Looks like half the school's here."

34

"More than half. Even some of the freshmen came," Morgan complained.

"Why shouldn't they?" Caitlin said innocently. "Dean Foster said it had to be an open party."

Morgan only frowned and shrugged. "At least we won't have to put up with them at the senior picnic next month."

"You were a freshman once, too, Morgan," Laurence noted. "Give them a break."

Ignoring his remark, Morgan motioned them toward the area lit by strings of lights in the trees. Caitlin glanced around, trying to convince herself she really wasn't looking for Jed. She didn't see him and breathed a sigh of relief. *So far, so good*, she thought. Maybe Jed had a school project that would keep him from coming.

"Good dance tape." The music was so loud that Laurence had to lean down and talk right in Caitlin's ear.

She smiled and nodded.

"You want to dance?" he asked.

"Sure, if you do."

Laurence took her arm and led her to an open spot on the brick pavement in front of a speaker. An expert dancer, Caitlin didn't feel the least bit self-conscious. As they started dancing, she willed herself to put everything from her mind but the music. Laurence seemed to be doing the

35

same, although when he looked at her, his eyes had a special glow.

They continued dancing for three more songs, the last of which was slow. Laurence held her close, then whispered in her ear, "This is nice. We'll have to do it more often."

She was lifting her face to smile at him when she saw Jed standing at the edge of the crowd watching them. Before she had a chance to read his expression, he turned and walked away through the crush of bodies. Her heart was pounding so hard she was sure Laurence would hear it hammering, but he didn't seem to notice anything wrong.

Caitlin tried to force her heart to slow down to a normal beat, but it was impossible because all she could see in her mind was Jed's face. She was relieved when Laurence suggested they take a break after the song ended.

"Do you want a soda?" he asked, still holding her hand.

"Sure. Dancing made me thirsty," she answered, knowing the refreshment table was in the opposite direction from where Jed had gone. Safely away from him for a few minutes, she took a long drink from the can of soda Laurence handed her.

They weren't alone for long. In a minute Ginny and Bert squeezed over to them.

"The whole school must be here!" Ginny exclaimed. "I feel as if somebody put me in a sardine can."

"What do you mean? It's fun," Caitlin said. "Have you and Bert been dancing?"

"And risk breaking my toes? No way."

"You take a bigger risk on the hunt course," Caitlin reminded her lightly.

"Yeah, but out there there's only Cinnamon and me." After a short pause, Ginny shrugged. "I don't know, I suppose I could give it a try. What do you say, Bert?"

"I thought you'd never ask."

"Just don't step on my toes!" Ginny lightly jabbed an elbow into her boyfriend's ribs. "Or I'm not riding with you at Appleveil." She glanced to Caitlin. "Is your grandmother riding?"

The Appleveil Hunt opened the Virginia season, and since she'd been old enough to stay in the saddle and join the adults, Caitlin had ridden with her grandmother. It was a fox hunt in true English tradition, held at a large estate, Appleveil, in the horse country surrounding Highgate. "You know Grandmother. You'd have to tie her down to keep her away," Caitlin replied.

"Caitlin, I've been looking all over for you!"

The four of them looked up to see Roger Wake, who'd walked over from the dance area.

"Oh, hi, Roger." Caitlin smiled. "Great party."

"Since you arranged it, of course." He laughed. "Listen, Caitlin, I can never get you alone for five minutes, but I've got to talk to you about the student council stuff for this year. Two big things." Roger was gesturing with his hands as he often did when he spoke. "First the fundraiser. I need an idea for a theme."

"So I heard," Caitlin said. "But, Roger, it's your job this year to come up with an idea."

"But I can't!" he said almost desperately. "And none of the other guys can either."

"Did you ever think of asking the *girls*?"

"Well, no," Roger said sheepishly. "But last year the girls ran the whole thing. This year I thought the boys should."

"Fine. Then you have to come up with your own idea." She glanced up at Laurence. "What do you think? Can you help him out?"

"I might be able to," Laurence said.

"Yeah?" Roger was full of hope. "What? What can beat a male beauty contest? And don't say a female one—that's been done a million times."

"Let me think about it," Laurence said. "Maybe we could get the faculty to join in this year and do a skit on something really funny. Why don't we get together at the dorm some night, and we'll talk about it."

"Great. Monday night?"

"You aren't desperate or anything, are you, Roger?" Caitlin giggled.

He cast her a black look, then remembered the second question he had to ask. "As you know, the senior class picnic is next month. Now, as student council president, this isn't my responsibility, but I am supposed to appoint a committee head to take care of it. I want you to be committee head."

"I don't know if I want to. Why don't you ask Morgan?"

"I figure you're more organized."

"Aren't you sweet." Caitlin tucked her long, black hair behind one ear and thought for a moment. "Well, my grandmother has a huge tract of mining land in the West Virginia mountains. It's not all that far from here. I can offer the spot, but I really can't be head of the committee. I'm just too busy this year," Caitlin insisted. "I've got Ian to work with and a pretty heavy schedule, and I'd like to get some riding in once in a while."

"Okay, okay. I'll ask Morgan. But at least see if you can get that place. It beats the state park where they've had the senior picnic for the last zillion years. And I already talked to Brett, his family doesn't want the whole class at their place at the lake."

"I'll talk to my grandmother and arrange it."

A slow song was playing, and Bert took hold of Ginny's arm. "I'll get her to dance," he promised as they disappeared.

"Come on over and talk to the other guys now so we can arrange a meeting," Roger suggested at that point, as much to Laurence as to Caitlin.

Roger led them through the ring of students milling around the dance area to the opposite side of the quad where some benches had been set out on the bricks and grass. "They're all over here," Roger called reassuringly. "Senior corner."

They broke through the crowd into a corner of the quad behind the old main building where several old oak trees branched out over the brick pavement. Most of the benches had been set out there, and the lights were strung from the tree branches overhead, almost making a roof.

Nearly all of Caitlin's closest friends were there, as well as some of the newer arrivals she didn't know that well. They were sitting on the benches or standing in groups, talking.

Morgan motioned them over. "Where have you been?" she asked Roger quietly, although there was a sharp edge to her voice.

"Talking, trying to get a committee together.

It's been decided you're going to be the head of the picnic committee."

"Why, thank you, Roger." She gave him a wide smile.

"I told him you were the best person for the job," Caitlin added.

"Caitlin's offered a spot on one of her grandmother's properties for the picnic," Roger explained.

Caitlin could see Morgan's eyes narrowing, so she laid a hand reassuringly on Morgan's shoulder. "They said they were tired of the state park, so I offered a place in West Virginia."

"What's it like, Caitlin?" Morgan continued. "A lot of mountains and pine trees?"

"I guess. I haven't been there in a while myself, not since I was six or seven. But I remember it being very green and pretty—"

Caitlin stopped suddenly. On the opposite row of benches under the trees, Caitlin spotted Jed. Her stomach sank. He was sitting on a bench between two girls, and another girl was standing beside them, talking. One of the girls was Tara; the others were sophomores. He was laughing and talking to them. He hadn't looked in Caitlin's direction; he didn't know she was there. As she studied him, she observed that he didn't seem particularly interested in any of the girls. But they were interested in *him*, hanging on to his every word.

Caitlin reached up and squeezed Laurence's hand. She felt a terrible compulsion to go over and talk to Jed, but she wouldn't. She forced herself to look away from him.

With one ear she listened to Roger and Laurence arranging a meeting with a couple of the other guys for Monday night. Then as other kids came over to their group, the talk turned to soccer.

"We've got a great team," Matt spoke confidently. "This year we can't miss!"

"With Roger and Jed as forwards, and almost the whole first squad returning," Tim chimed in, "not one of the other schools stands a chance."

"Right, Jed?" Matt yelled over to him.

Involuntarily, Caitlin glanced in Jed's direction, wincing as she saw Tara place a hand on his shoulder.

"Right," he shouted back and grinned. His pride for the team was clearly evident.

Although Jed smiled at the rest of the group, he pointedly avoided looking at Caitlin. It was as if she didn't exist. She leaned a little closer to Laurence and tried to act as if none of it mattered, that she didn't care that Jed couldn't even be her friend. But it was very obvious to her that he hadn't forgiven her and that he hated her as much as ever.

"Let's go dance again," she said to Laurence.

"Sure," Laurence agreed quickly. Whether or not he was aware of her reaction to seeing Jed, he said nothing about it as he took her arm and walked with her to the dance area.

Caitlin kept Laurence dancing through the next five songs. Laurence was leading her smoothly through a moody, slow song when she glanced to her side to see Jed and Tara dancing next to them. Jed's and Caitlin's eyes met for the first time in months. Caitlin managed a slight smile, and Jed returned it with a cold, hard stare. Then he looked away abruptly. If he'd slapped Caitlin in the face, his meaning couldn't have been more obvious. He acted as if he didn't even know her.

Not long after that, Caitlin coaxed Laurence into leaving the party. "I'm really tired, Laurence. Do you mind?"

"No. I've had enough myself. I'll walk you back."

Caitlin didn't even wait to say good night to any of the others. It was all she could do to hold back the tears that kept welling up in her eyes. On the pretense of wanting to go right up to bed, she told Laurence she couldn't even talk.

"I'll see you in the morning," she whispered after he'd kissed her good night.

"I'll be here about nine." He smiled.

"Good." Without looking back she hurried inside and up the stairs to her room.

She knew, even as she walked away, that she was being unfair to Laurence. She didn't *want* to be that way. She cared about him, but whenever memories of Jed filled her thoughts, she knew she didn't give Laurence the attention he deserved. Why did that have to happen? Why couldn't she be as sweet and kind to him as he was to her? It made her feel terrible. Oh, God, she thought, was she going to make a mess of everything in her life?

5

Caitlin had just returned to the dorm late the next morning after riding with Laurence, when Mrs. Chaney, the dorm mother, called her to the telephone. Caitlin had barely slept the night before, and it had taken most of her remaining energy to cover up her tiredness. Her voice was weary as she went across the hall and picked up the phone.

"Hello."

"Hello, dear."

"Oh, hi, Grandmother."

"I'm leaving for New York tomorrow for a few days on mining business," Mrs. Ryan said. "I should be back by Thursday. I'm planning to invite the Baxters for dinner the weekend after next. I want you to bring Laurence, of course."

"Fine." Caitlin was too tired to challenge her

grandmother. Although she didn't mind having dinner with Laurence's parents, she hated the way her grandmother demanded her attendance.

"By the way," Regina Ryan said after a moment's pause, "have you heard from Dr. Westlake recently?"

Caitlin was startled by the question. "Not since I've been back at school." Before school started, he had written Caitlin two letters and sent them to Ryan Acres, but her grandmother knew about that.

"He hasn't stopped calling me. My secretary tells me he called twice this week alone. I haven't returned his calls, of course, but I wondered whether he was trying to get in touch with you."

"He'd better not," Caitlin stated firmly. "I told him I didn't want anything to do with him."

"Very well," Regina Ryan said smoothly, the point settled to her satisfaction. "I'll call when I get back from New York. Good-bye, dear."

"Good-bye, Grandmother." After she'd hung up the receiver, Caitlin stood for several seconds staring at the phone. Her grandmother's words left her uneasy. Why couldn't her father leave her alone? What did he want? Would he really come to the school to try to talk to her? Well, if he did, Caitlin had no intention of speaking to him.

* * *

For the rest of the weekend, Caitlin avoided seeing Jed again, and that helped ease some of the hurt she'd experienced at the dance. On Saturday night she and Laurence and some of the others got together in the girl's dorm lounge to watch videos, and on Sunday she and Laurence took a long drive through the Virginia countryside in Caitlin's shining red car. The car had been a gift from her grandmother the previous June, and she loved it. The Nissan ZX was her ticket to getting out and away when she had to, or wanted to. They stopped for hamburgers in Middleburg and drove back to campus just as the sun was setting over the mountains.

Caitlin went to the Fosters' the next few afternoons, determined to break through Ian's wall of fear and get him to want to walk again. But his progress was agonizingly slow. Although he put up with the exercises for his legs, he never made the effort to attempt to walk.

"Come on, Ian, just one more stretch," Caitlin coaxed one afternoon. She was pushing for a few more exercises each day, strengthening Ian's legs in degrees that wouldn't be so painful to him, yet would still get results.

"I'm tired, Caitlin. It hurts!" he cried.

"You're almost in the castle. You're going to beat me."

Her words gave him the incentive to allow her to move his legs in one more set of knee bends and stretches.

"There, that wasn't so bad!" she called out. "Come on, I'll help you into your chair."

Ian's relief was almost visible. He was barely seated in the wheelchair before he was already studying the game board. He'd obviously already made up his mind.

"I want to move the black knight into the castle."

"Great." Caitlin laughed. "You win."

Ian giggled. "Even if you lose, it doesn't matter. We'll still be best friends."

Caitlin felt the tears coming to her eyes. "Of course we will, Ian. This is only a game."

"Right." He nodded his blond head, then gave her an impish smile. "If it was a real treasure, Caitlin, I'd share it with you."

She fought to keep her voice light. "If it was a real treasure, what would you do with it, Ian?"

"Oh, go to the candy store and buy candy for a year, and ice cream. And I'd get a Ferrari, but you'd have to drive it. Then we could take a jet plane to some of those places you told me about, like Africa and that place where they have all the sailboats. I could go fishing. Dad used to take me fishing last year. I caught a trout. Did I tell you?" His eyes were sparkling. "This big." He extended his hands to the size of a fish that would have weighed in at at least fifteen pounds.

It took all of Caitlin's willpower to hold back her tears. How could this little boy love her so much, when all she'd done to deserve it was to try to make up for the damage she'd caused? "That's some fish," she finally managed to say. "I used to go fishing, too, with the gardener at my grandmother's house. But I never caught anything much bigger than this." She extended her hands about six inches apart.

Ian laughed. "Maybe Dad can take us fishing sometime, and I could teach you how."

"Great! I'll even put the worms on myself."

"That's the easy part," he said scornfully.

When Caitlin left the Fosters' late that afternoon, she was feeling more guilty than ever. She'd won a little boy's love, but under false pretenses, and she couldn't pretend to herself it was anything but that.

She was doing all she could, she told herself. The Fosters were quick to tell her that she was making more progress with Ian than the staff of professionals at the summer school had been able to.

It wasn't enough, though. It would never be enough.

On her way back to the dormitory, she ran into Morgan, the last person she wanted to see at that moment.

"I'm glad I saw you." Morgan had that mischievous look in her eyes that usually meant some juicy gossip was coming. "You'll never guess what I heard today."

"What?" Caitlin answered mechanically, only half listening.

"Guess who asked whom to a weekend party at her parents' house in Washington?" She paused tantalizingly. "And guess who accepted?"

"I wouldn't know, Morgan. I have other things to do besides listen to the latest gossip."

"Tara and Jed," Morgan announced. "And he's spending the entire weekend at her house."

It took all of Caitlin's willpower not to show her reaction to the news. "Interesting," she said lightly. "But I don't know why you think I'd care."

"Cute, Caitlin. I saw you looking at Jed at the party."

"I looked at a lot of people. I also noticed Roger looking at a lot of people, including Jane Winthrop."

Caitlin's shot hit home. For an instant Morgan stiffened, then relaxed. "I know where I stand with Roger. Jane doesn't mean a thing to him."

"Believe what you want."

"I'm only telling you this so you know what some girls in this school will do—"

Caitlin cut Morgan short. "Tara can do whatever she pleases. The last time I saw her and Jed at the party, he wasn't exactly hanging all over her."

"You *do* still care! I knew it!" Morgan exclaimed. "What happened between you two, anyway?"

"Nothing, and I don't particularly care what he does anymore."

"Not even going to Washington with Tara? That's got to mean something," Morgan speculated slyly.

"Morgan"—Caitlin's patience had reached an end—"I know it's hard for you, but try not to be such a pain. Jed and I are a thing of the past, all right? Now leave me alone!"

With that, she walked quickly away. Storming into her dorm a minute later, Caitlin flung her bag on the bed.

Ginny looked up from the desk, where she was working on her homework. "What happened?"

"Oh, that Morgan," Caitlin fumed. "Sometimes she can be such a jerk!"

Ginny hid her grin, knowing Morgan only too well. "What did she do now?"

"You know how she's always trying to get me to talk about why Jed and I broke up?" Caitlin placed her hands on her hips and faced Ginny. "Just now she came running over to me as I was walking back from the Fosters'." Caitlin angrily mimicked Morgan's tone. "'Guess who's asked whom to a weekend party? And guess who's accepted?' she asked. I told her I had better things to do than listen to gossip, so, of course, she had to tell me what I didn't want to hear— that Tara's asked Jed to a party at her parents' house in Washington and he's accepted! Damn her." Caitlin opened the refrigerator and took out a diet soda. "She must know I don't want to hear anything about Jed, but she's got to rub it in. Doesn't she have any feelings?"

"Not where gossip's concerned," Ginny said dryly. "Last year she got me really upset telling me Bert was hanging out with Lacey Whitaker. Turned out it wasn't even true. What she said today probably isn't either."

"Whether it's true or not, doesn't she ever think before she opens her mouth? No," Caitlin answered her own question. "I believe she *was* thinking. She was trying to get me angry enough so that I'd let something slip about Jed and me. Then she'd really have something to gossip about!"

"Did you?"

"No, of course not. But, Ginny, it still hurts. I don't want to hear about Tara and Jed seeing each other. I don't even want to think about it, but now I have to."

"They may not be. How did she find out, anyway?"

"I didn't ask her."

"Well," Ginny said consoling her, "I'll bet she didn't hear it from Jed, and I haven't noticed that she's an especially good friend of Tara's."

"You know what I'm going to do?" Caitlin said decisively. "I'm going to avoid her—totally! Maybe then she'll get the message." Caitlin chuckled to herself. "I'll even tell her I've given her place at the table to someone else. Won't that get her! I can't wait to see her expression."

Ginny giggled, too. "I wouldn't mind seeing her expression, either, though I hate to say it would only give her something else to talk about."

"But no one *important* would be listening." Caitlin smiled to herself as she considered her revenge. At least it gave her something else to think about besides Tara and Jed spending a weekend together.

Yet as she lay in bed before falling asleep that night, she realized that snubbing Morgan was a petty thing—it wouldn't solve what was really bothering her. It wouldn't bring Jed back.

6

Thursday night after dinner Caitlin went to the library to research an English literature paper that was due the next week. She'd chosen the Brontë sisters to profile, and she needed additional biographical information.

As Caitlin crossed the lawns of the campus toward the main building, where the library was housed, other students were strolling along the brick walkways or sitting in groups on the lush grass, enjoying the long evening twilight. She waved to several friends along the way but didn't stop to talk.

As Caitlin entered the library she noticed that the only other person there was the assistant librarian, who was seated at her desk, looking through some papers. Highgate's well-endowed library contained a far better selection than most of the local town libraries. Several thousand volumes filled the wooden floor-to-ceiling shelves in two rooms, and there was additional research material in the closed stacks kept in the basement. Caitlin went directly to the biographical section and chose two books, one on the Brontës and the other on nineteenth-century female writers.

With books and notebook in hand, Caitlin went into the old drawing room where study tables and soft chairs were set up near a marble fireplace and tall windows. She lost track of time as she read and jotted down bits of information in her notebook. After she had scanned the pages of the Brontë biography, she realized she needed more information about Emily. Caitlin had noticed a passing mention in the biography that Emily had described to her sisters the visions she'd had that had inspired her to write *Wuthering Heights*. Intrigued, Caitlin glanced through the appendix for the biographer's reference materials. There was another, much older biography listed, so she decided to see if the library had it in the closed stacks.

Carrying the book with her, Caitlin went to the card catalog and, to her delight, found a listing for the older book. Quickly she jotted down the reference number and returned the card drawer to its proper slot. In her excitement, she stepped quickly around the card catalog case and walked right into a student approaching from the other direction.

"Jed!" The word was a startled whisper.

She thought for an instant he wasn't going to acknowledge her at all, but then he said coldly, "You ought to look where you're going, Caitlin."

"I—I found a book I was looking for," she said dumbly. "I guess I was in a hurry."

He glared at her, whatever emotions he was feeling masked behind his expressionless face. Caitlin, however, felt her knees turn to water at his sudden nearness. A moment later Jed began to turn away.

"Jed," she cried quietly in panic. She felt a need to do something to get through that cold, invisible wall separating them. "Can't you even talk to me?"

He looked back at her. "What is there to say?" he rasped.

"Anything," she pleaded. "You treat me as if you hardly even know me. You never told me why you walked out last year."

"You mean you haven't figured that out yet? Come on, Caitlin. You're not stupid."

"Why won't you give me a chance to explain?"

"So you could con me again, like you conned everyone else?"

"I was going to tell you everything. That's why I wrote that letter."

"But you didn't give it to me. I had to find it by accident. Meanwhile, you let Diana suffer for six months while you were out having a good time."

"I've been trying to make up for that." There were tears in her huge blue eyes.

Jed wasn't moved. "Sure. When Diana was nearly dead, you did your little good deed and ran over to the hospital to help her."

"There's a lot more to it than that!"

"You still haven't told the Fosters you were to blame, have you?" he accused in a cutting whisper. "You're over there like a guardian angel, pretending to be so concerned—and even *I* bought that act last year," he added bitterly. "But it's not concern that drives you, is it? It's guilt—rotten, stinking guilt, and you're too much of a coward to admit it."

"That's not so!" But even as she denied it, she knew there was some truth to his accusation. "I know how wrong I was. I'm trying to undo all the damage I've done. I've learned a lesson. I've changed!"

"People don't change that much."

"But I have!"

"You made a fool out of me once and hurt a lot of other innocent people. Maybe Diana can forgive you, but I can't." Caitlin could see him closing himself to her again. "I don't have anything else to say to you."

Tears were streaming down Caitlin's cheeks. "Please. I'm so sorry for everything I did. I've done everything I can to make up for it. Jed, I still love you. I can't stand the way you're treating me. Can't we even be friends?"

For an instant Jed's expression softened. Grasping at the slim sign of hope, Caitlin gazed up at him, her lips trembling. "Please, can't you give me another chance? I'll tell the Fosters. I'll do *anything*!" She reached a hand toward him.

As he stared down at her, his face suddenly froze, and the muscles in his neck tightened. "Find another sucker, Caitlin," he said icily.

With that, he swung away from her, grabbed his books from a nearby table, and walked quickly out of the library without a backward glance.

Caitlin breathed deeply to stop the sob that was climbing up her throat. She hurt as she'd never hurt in her life.

In a daze she went back to the study table to collect her bag and other books. Not fully conscious of what she was doing, she replaced the two books she'd taken from the shelves. She still held the piece of paper with the reference number written on it. Mechanically, she walked to the librarian's desk and handed her the paper.

"This book, please." Her voice was lifeless.

"That'll take a second." The librarian smiled. "I have to go downstairs."

Caitlin nodded, staring out the back window of the building toward the boy's dorms. She felt drained and numb and full of pain. She wished she could blank out the last few minutes and pretend they had never happened. But she knew that was impossible, just as it was impossible to turn back the clock to the day of Ian's accident and change the horror of that.

Accepting the book the librarian handed her a few minutes later, Caitlin turned and walked out of the building across the quad. It registered in a corner of her mind that she was supposed to be going back to the dorm to study, but she didn't want to have to face Ginny and the rest of her friends. She just continued walking until she reached the stables at the far end of the campus.

It was nearly dark, and the stables were deserted. Dropping her books on the bench outside Duster's stall, she unlatched the door and went inside. Duster nickered in greeting, and Caitlin softly patted his neck.

"We're going for a ride, boy," she whispered, hearing her voice crack and tremble with unshed tears. Once before, she'd saddled up and ridden out in a similar state—the morning at Ryan Acres when she'd read the details of Ian's accident in the paper and realized she'd been the one responsible for leaving the maintenance shed door unlocked and spilling the chemicals that Ian had later eaten. It had been raining that day, a torrential downpour, and she'd already been coming down with a cold. But she'd ridden into the storm, half hoping it would cleanse her from the terrible guilt she'd felt. She didn't even remember returning from the ride, having been only semiconscious from a high fever that had kept her bedridden for a week. By the time she'd recovered, Diana had already left Highgate in shame, and Caitlin felt it was best to keep quiet about her role in the tragedy. *Oh, how wrong I was*, she thought sadly as she untied Duster. As painful as it would have been for her to confess the truth then, she realized it would have been nothing compared to the terrible grief she felt now.

Caitlin led Duster out of the stall and put him in crossties as she went to collect his saddle and bridle. Quickly she tacked him up, then led him outside.

There was a sliver of moon in the sky and enough dusky light to enable her to see the path from the stable leading to the meadows beyond. Latching the paddock gate behind her, she mounted Duster and turned toward the path.

Duster's ears were flicking back and forth, and he snorted uneasily as he adjusted to the darkness. Caitlin had never taken him out after nightfall before. She didn't feel any of his uneasiness, though. All she knew was that she wanted to ride and feel the wind in her hair, blowing against her face, sweeping the pain away.

Once her own eyes had adjusted to the darkness, she heeled Duster into a trot away from the stable. She knew nearly every inch of the riding trails and meadows by heart and guided Duster with a firm, assured pressure on the reins. When they reached the open, rolling grassland, she immediately heeled him to a canter. The horse, too, had finally adjusted to the darkness. Across the dry September grass they cantered, then galloped. With Caitlin's long hair streaming behind, they made a striking gray-black silhouette in the pale moonlight.

Caitlin rode all over the miles of meadows and pastures around Highgate, stopping only to unlatch gates where necessary. Jumping the fences would have been easier, but she had enough presence of mind not to take that risk with Duster in the darkness.

They were totally alone out in the meadows. The wind whipped at Caitlin's face as they covered the ground in huge strides. In those moments, Caitlin felt freer than she had in weeks. She could wipe everything from her mind as the wind was drying the tears from her cheeks. Highgate, Ryan Acres, and all the pain she'd encountered at both belonged to another world. She didn't need Jed's love now, she didn't need her grandmother's, or the support of a father who'd deserted her in infancy. Even the crushing guilt of being the cause of Ian's and Diana's suffering was blissfully, if only temporarily, forgotten.

Only when Duster began to slow the pace himself, did Caitlin turn him back toward the Highgate stables. Her pain was only a dull throb now. She never would be able to forget the look on Jed's face or the cold rejection of his words to her that night. But she could bury them; she could hide them away with all the other pain she'd suffered.

Caitlin had no idea what time it was when they arrived back at the stables. Duster was lathered up, though, and she wasn't going to neglect him. After loosening his saddle girth, she walked him for twenty minutes around the paddock until his belly and chest felt cool, then she unsaddled and unbridled him, put on his halter, and clipped him into the crossties in the barn. With a bucket of lukewarm water, she sponged him down, then worked a sweat strap over his coat, removing the excess water. Toweling Duster dry, she brushed him, and to ensure he wouldn't get a chill, she buckled a lightweight blanket over him. Then she put him in his stall, checking both his feed and water.

Before leaving, she wrapped an arm around Duster's neck and pressed her cheek to his sleek, black coat. "Thanks, boy. It was a wonderful ride. Thanks for always being there."

Duster whinnied quietly.

"Tomorrow I'll bring you a bag of carrots. I'll drive to Martinsville to get some."

Closing the stall door, she tiredly picked up the saddle and bridle and returned them to the tack room. Then she retrieved her books from the bench and walked out into the night air back toward the dorm.

Caitlin's feet left a trail in the dew-covered grass as she climbed the hill, and the bottom edges of her tight-legged jeans grew damp. She thought that her ankles would probably be chafed in the morning from riding so hard without boots, though she didn't notice any soreness at the moment.

It was with reluctance that she climbed the stone steps of the dorm building before going inside. She could have spent all night out under the cloudless, star-spattered sky where there was freedom. Going inside meant a return to everything that hurt her.

But when Caitlin turned the handle, the door was locked. That meant it was past the ten o'clock curfew. What was she going to do?

Quickly Caitlin ran to the back of the two-story brick dorm building to see if Ginny was still awake. She sighed with relief when she noticed the light still glowing in their room.

Caitlin reached down into the flower bed surrounding the building and searched for some pebbles. Finding a few, she tossed one at the window directly over Ginny's bed. She heard the click as the stone bounced against the glass. But there was no response from inside. She continued to throw stones until finally she saw Ginny's face peering out the window.

"What's going on?" Ginny called out nervously.

"Ginny, it's me, Caitlin. I'm locked out. Let me in."

"Caitlin, I've been worried sick about you. Where have you been?"

"I'll tell you later. Just let me in."

"Okay. Go around to the front."

Caitlin raced back to the front door and in a minute heard the lock release from inside.

"Hurry up before Mrs. Chaney catches us," Ginny whispered.

Once they were safely in their room, Ginny turned to her roommate. "Okay, now tell me. Where were you? When you didn't get back by nine, I went to the library looking for you."

"I went for a ride."

"In the dark? Are you crazy? What happened?"

"Nothing I want to talk about."

"Come on. It must have been something pretty awful. You'd be better off telling someone about it."

"I don't want to talk," Caitlin insisted.

"Were you with Laurence?"

"No. I was by myself."

"Caitlin, I've only seen you looking this bad once before. It has something to do with Jed, doesn't it?"

Caitlin lowered her eyes but didn't answer.

"You'll feel better if you tell me. Did you see him tonight?"

Without a word, Caitlin walked mechanically to the closet and removed her nightgown and robe from their hooks. Clutching them, she walked over to her bed. The burden of carrying all her feelings was finally too much for her, however, and as soon as she sat down on her bed, she burst into tears. "Oh, God, it was so awful, Ginny." She gulped back a sob.

Ginny immediately sat down on the bed beside Caitlin and put an arm around Caitlin's shoulders. "What happened?"

"I—I saw Jed in the library. I—I tried to talk to him, to tell him I was sorry. But he said such terrible things to me—" She shuddered uncontrollably, unable to calm down despite Ginny's efforts to console her.

"What did he say?" Ginny prodded.

"He told me to find another sucker. He told me he could never forgive me."

"Forgive you for what?" As Caitlin continued to sob, Ginny added softly, "I want to understand, Caitlin. I want to help you. But I can't unless you tell me the real reason you two broke up."

"Oh, Ginny," Caitlin said with a choked voice. "I did something awful, but I've been trying so hard to make up for it."

"What could you have done that was so awful?"

Caitlin shook her head. "If I tell you, you'll hate me," she said.

"You ought to know me better than that by now. I could never hate you, Caitlin."

Caitlin looked up at her friend and saw the love and caring in her own misty eyes. She realized she had to risk telling Ginny the truth; she couldn't hold it inside any longer. She took a deep breath to calm herself. "Ginny, I'm the one who's responsible for Ian's accident. I left the shed unlocked that day."

Ginny stared at her friend, unable to hold back her shock. "My God," she gasped.

"I didn't mean to. It was an accident," she continued.

"Of course it was," Ginny said, recovering from the news. "You don't think anyone would believe you did it intentionally, do you?"

Caitlin shook her head, the tears flowing freely. "I didn't know what to believe. I was getting a pitchfork to use as a prop for the fund-raiser and just forgot to lock the door again. I wasn't thinking about it. My mind had been on Jed and Diana. You remember how interested he was in her at the time—"

"Poor Diana," Ginny whispered. "Everybody thought she did it. Why didn't you tell anybody then?"

"I didn't even know what had happened until two weeks later when I read the report of the police investigation in the paper. Ginny, I was so scared. I kept making excuses not to tell. Then I told myself that it probably wouldn't make a difference even if I did confess. Diana had left school, and I figured it didn't matter any longer who was to blame."

"How could you, Caitlin?"

"I wasn't thinking straight. But as soon as I found out how much I'd hurt Diana, I realized how wrong I was. I haven't had a moment's peace since this all began. I've been trying to do all I can to make up for it, but nothing works. I've cause so much pain to so many people."

"Caitlin." Ginny wrapped her arms around her friend. "You've been suffering all this time, too. Everything's starting to make sense to me now. Your work with Ian and with Diana at the hospital this summer—"

"I thought if I could help make them well again, it would right at least some of the wrong I'd done. I told Diana the truth, and it helped her to recover. She forgave me, Ginny. I only wish Jed could, too."

"So that's why he broke up with you," Ginny said. She shook her head. "I would have thought he would have been more understanding, realizing how hard it was for you to tell him."

"I didn't tell him," Caitlin admitted. "Oh, not that I didn't try a thousand times. When we first started dating, I even wrote a letter to him, confessing everything. But I was scared and never gave it to him. He made me feel so special and loved, Ginny, and I was afraid if I told him the truth he'd leave me. So I put the letter in a book and forgot all about it until the day he helped move my stuff home for the summer. The book with the letter in it fell out of a box, and I stashed it in the glove compartment of my car. Somehow Jed found it. But he didn't say anything to me until prom night. And then"—Caitlin paused, trying to control the tears that streamed down her cheeks at the memory of that night—"he acted so horribly to me. One minute he was nice, the next he was cold. He never said anything about the letter or what happened. He just told me over and over again how I'd made a fool out of him and what a cold, manipulative person I was. At the time I didn't know what he was talking about. But he'd suddenly turned into someone I didn't know. He grabbed my arms and was really rough. He tried to force himself on me, but stopped himself. Then he left me at Brett's house—alone. I felt so confused and miserable. I didn't discover that he'd found the letter until Diana talked to him this summer."

"It must have been a shock to him," Ginny reasoned. "Especially since you shared everything else with him."

"I know, Ginny, and if the tables were turned I'm not sure I wouldn't have acted the same way. What I did was awful, and I should have to suffer for it. But I still love Jed, and the way he's treating me is too much for me to handle. He won't forgive me or try to understand at all. He hates me now, Ginny, and I don't know what to do."

For a minute Ginny was silent, letting Caitlin

cry on her shoulder. Then she spoke. "I wish I knew what to tell you about Jed. But nothing I can say will bring him back or make him understand. I do know that you're never going to rid yourself of your guilt until you stop carrying this burden around inside you. You've got to tell everyone the truth about the accident. Does anybody else know?"

"Just Laurence," she admitted.

"What about the Fosters?"

Caitlin shook her head no.

"Then they still blame Diana. Caitlin, you know that's not fair to her or to them."

"Diana thought it would be best if I didn't say anything, but I think you're right. I do want to tell them. It's just that I'm doing so well with Ian. If I tell them, I'm sure they won't let me see him anymore."

"You don't know that for a fact," Ginny argued. "But I think you'll have to take that chance."

The worst of Caitlin's sobs had subsided, but she was still trembling. "I will tell them. I promise," she said.

"It may make a difference to Jed, too," Ginny added.

Caitlin gave her friend a quick hug and managed a tiny smile. "I don't know what I'd do without you, Ginny," she said.

It would take more than Ginny's friendship to ease her mind, Caitlin thought as she struggled to sleep that night. But did she really have the courage to tell the Fosters she was the one who had ruined their son's life?

7

The following Tuesday, Caitlin looked up from the English literature paper she was writing at her desk. "Ginny, how'd you like to come to Ryan Acres for the weekend?" she asked.

Ginny had already finished her homework and was leafing through the latest issue of *Horse and Rider*. She turned to Caitlin, her brow furrowed in thought. "This weekend? Sure, what's up?"

"Oh, nothing special." Absently Caitlin twirled her pen in her fingers. "I told Grandmother I was coming out, and Laurence and his parents are coming Saturday afternoon for a ride and then dinner." Caitlin was feeling a little better than she had a few days earlier, but just the same, she wanted the company of her friend during the time Laurence wouldn't be at Ryan Acres.

"A riding weekend, huh?" Ginny instantly looked more alert. "Great. I'll definitely come. Has your grandmother got the jump course set out?"

Caitlin nodded. "She had Jeff and the other stable hands set up the jumps in the back pasture. That's the only place where they can rig a water jump."

Ginny grinned. "Who are you going to let me ride?"

"How about Apris? I tried her out at the end of the summer. Jeff's got her really well schooled, and she's a good fencer—though a little green and strong headed."

"She sounds like she's right up my alley. I'll ride her. When are we leaving?"

"Friday after last class—that is, unless you've got something planned with Bert Friday night."

"No. He's going away to a debate tournament Friday afternoon." Ginny paused a moment before adding, "It'll be good to see your grandmother, too. It's been awhile."

Caitlin went back to her paper without replying. She'd never told Ginny, but she'd always believed her grandmother felt more of a kinship with Ginny than with her. She always asked about her and welcomed her to Ryan Acres with open arms. Often it was more than she offered Caitlin.

Caitlin saw Jed more than she would have liked that week. On Wednesday, as she passed the soccer field on her way to the stables, she couldn't resist looking down the hill to the level field. She picked Jed out immediately from the other uniformed players. He was practicing shots on the goal while the majority of the other players were grouped together, talking. Without even seeing his face, she easily recognized his lithe, well-muscled body. Quickly she looked the other way.

She saw him in the dining room the next day as well. Although Tara was right behind him in the lunch line, he didn't seem to be paying attention to her. He picked up his food tray and walked to a table where several of his soccer teammates were seated. Immediately he joined in on their spirited conversation.

Caitlin looked back to the lunch line to watch Tara's reactions. The girl stared after Jed with the look of someone who was very hurt and bewildered. Finally she picked up her tray and walked to a table not far away from the soccer players.

As Tara sat down, Jed looked up, but not at

her. His glance was quick and sidelong at Caitlin's table, where she sat with Ginny, Gloria, and Jessica, who'd been invited to join them earlier in the week. That had left a clearly angered Morgan no choice but to find a seat at another table. Jed turned away quickly, back to the boys' conversation.

Laurence came up in the interim, leaning over Caitlin's shoulder and picking up the apple from her tray.

"Do you want to sit down?" she asked. "Gloria's leaving."

"No," he answered, smiling as he bit into the apple, "I just wanted to say hello. I'll get a sandwich and eat it on the way over to the lab. I'm working on a chemistry project."

"Do me a favor and blow up the lab so I don't have to suffer the rest of the year with Mr. Gladdings," Caitlin said, winking.

"No way. I like chemistry, remember?"

"Then maybe you could whip up a magic potion to make me like it, too," she said.

"I'll try. Maybe I'll bring some with me when I see you tonight." He dropped the apple back in her hand. "I'll meet you at your dorm about six-thirty."

"Great."

"I'll see you then." Gently Laurence squeezed her shoulder and left.

Caitlin looked across at the table where Jed was sitting to find him watching her again. Immediately he looked away.

Caitlin decided it was time for her to leave as well. It hurt more than ever to see Jed and feel his snubs. It was almost like hearing every one of his words of rejection all over again. "I've got to get going," she told her friends. "I have to stop at the library."

Gracefully hoisting her bag over her shoulder, and with the apple still in her hand, Caitlin began walking out of the dining room, which meant walking past the table where Jed sat.

She stared straight ahead as she passed. But her escape wasn't that easy. Tim called out, "Can't you even say hello, Caitlin?"

She had to turn, but she refused to look at Jed. "Oh, hi, Tim," she said, focusing her eyes only on him. "Sorry, guess I'm in a daze. I've got to get to the library. Good luck at the game this afternoon."

"Aren't you coming? It's a home game," Tim said.

"I can't. I'm baby-sitting for Ian, but I know you guys are going to win."

"We'd do even better with a few fans," Matt called out. "Especially you."

"Next time—I promise. Right now, I've really got to go. See you later." She had to get away.

She could almost feel the glare of Jed's gaze burning into the side of her face.

Late the following afternoon Caitlin turned her red Nissan ZX into the long, tree-lined drive of Ryan Acres. Both sides of the drive were graced with white-fenced paddocks and grazing Thoroughbreds.

Caitlin braked the sports car to a stop before the magnificent double door of the house. The days were growing shorter, and the double sconces on each side of the door were already lit as the butler-chauffeur, Rollins, ran down from the doorway.

"Good to see you, Miss Caitlin. I'll get the bags for you."

"Thanks, Rollins. You remember Ginny?"

"Yes, indeed. How are you, miss?"

"Good," Ginny answered.

Caitlin slipped out from behind the wheel. "Is my grandmother home?"

"In her study," Rollins answered.

"Ginny will stay in my room, Rollins," Caitlin instructed, then turned to her friend. "Come on in. We'll say hello to Grandmother first. Then we can change and relax a bit before dinner."

The two girls climbed the stone stairs and stepped into the marble-floored entrance hall.

Ginny had been to Ryan Acres many times before, and both she and Caitlin were too used to the elegant furnishings and fine paintings to take any special notice of them. Caitlin led Ginny down the hall toward her grandmother's study.

Regina Ryan was coming out of the room as they approached. She looked slim and elegant in an expensively tailored suit. Her silvery gray hair was perfectly styled in a short, swept-back cut that emphasized her high, patrician cheekbones. "I thought I heard voices. Hello, dear." She extended her cheek for Caitlin's kiss.

Mrs. Ryan turned to Ginny and clasped her hands warmly. "How good to see you, Ginny. I'm delighted you came."

"Hello, Mrs. Ryan." Ginny smiled.

"And how is your family?"

"Dad's off in the Middle East, trying to put out some diplomatic fire. Mom's fine, minding the store back in D.C."

"You'll be riding with us tomorrow, of course?" Mrs. Ryan inquired.

"Yes," Ginny said. "Caitlin thought I might like to try Apris. I hear she's quite spirited."

"Excellent idea, Caitlin." Regina Ryan nodded to her granddaughter, a gesture that made Caitlin do a double take. It was so unusual for her grandmother to pay her a compliment.

"Apris is ready for a rider like Ginny and a full day out," Regina Ryan went on. She released Ginny's hands and surveyed both girls, who were dressed in jeans and casual tops. "Well, you'll both want to wash and change before dinner. I thought we'd eat in the rear sitting room—it's much cozier than the dining room." She quickly checked her gold-and-diamond Rolex. "We'll meet in half an hour. Oh, and, Caitlin, I've been looking through some of those college brochures you sent me. We'll talk about them at dinner." She frowned before she turned and walked back toward her study.

Caitlin waited until she and Ginny were climbing the sweeping staircase to the second floor and safely out of earshot before speaking. "I didn't like that look she just gave me. I wonder what she's going to say about the colleges I chose. Never mind, I think I already know. She's going to say none of them is the proper place for me to learn how to run the family business."

"She's still trying to get you ready to take over Ryan Mining when she retires?" Ginny asked.

"You've got it. But I hate business, Ginny—anything to do with numbers and percentages and cost factors and all those things Grandmother talks about all the time. Why won't she let me just take liberal arts courses and figure out what I really want to do?"

"You don't know yet that she won't," Ginny commented.

"Spoken like a true diplomat's daughter, Ginny."

"And the last thing Dad wants me to do is follow in his footsteps," Ginny noted.

Caitlin sighed. "You're lucky. Just from the sound of her voice, I think she's going to say something like, 'I don't think you should consider any college but an Ivy League one. Where's Radcliffe's brochure?' or 'With your grades, you should be applying to Yale,'" Caitlin mimicked.

"Hey, what about a compromise—like Brown? I hear they've got a good liberal arts program," Ginny said encouragingly.

"That's a good idea. I forgot about Brown."

The girls had reached the landing and started down one of the Turkish runners covering the polished wood of the upstairs hallways.

"But she'll want me to major in business."

"So minor in something else you're interested in."

"But the point is, Ginny, that I don't want to take over Ryan Mining, and that's what she's pushing me toward. She likes you, and you get along with her. Be on my side at dinner tonight, okay?"

"Don't worry about it."

A few minutes later the girls entered Caitlin's huge bedroom, with its dusty rose carpeting, twin canopy beds, antique furnishings, fireplace, and chaise longue upholstered in a rose color to match the carpeting. The maid had already unpacked their overnight bags, and Caitlin motioned to the wall of closets in the connecting dressing room and bath. "Margaret probably put your things in there. Try the left side."

Caitlin went to the opposite side of the closet and extracted a stylish but conservative beige silk blouse and skirt that she knew her grandmother would like. Then, hanging the clothes on the back of the door, she walked into the bathroom and went across to the double marble sinks set under a sweep of mirrors. She turned on the taps.

Ginny came into the bathroom as Caitlin was wiping the cleansing cream off her face.

"Is that the secret of your perfect complexion?" she teased.

Caitlin frowned at her as she patted her face dry with a towel. "The beauty consultant in New York said it's never too early to stop using soap on your face."

"Whatever you say." Ginny shrugged, liberally lathering a bar of soap in her hands.

"You know you really shouldn't do that, Ginny," Caitlin reproved. "It may not matter now, but when you hit thirty and all the wrinkles start—"

Ginny laughed. "I'll never get old."

The two girls finished dressing and were downstairs within the half hour Mrs. Ryan had allotted them. Caitlin led the way toward the small sitting room at the back corner of the house behind the library. It was a comfortable room, and she was glad her grandmother had chosen it for their dinner that evening. The room was done in greens and pale golds and opened out onto the glass-enclosed conservatory, which was filled with flowering tropical plants. Because of the warmth of the evening, the conservatory doors were open.

Caitlin and Ginny had barely entered the room when Regina Ryan stepped in behind them. "My, you both look very nice this evening," she said. She walked toward the conservatory, then turned. "Caitlin, have you seen how well the orchids are doing? Come, take a look."

Caitlin and Ginny both followed Mrs. Ryan into the conservatory, where she motioned to the three tiers of orchid plants, most of which were in bloom. "I never thought when Barnes suggested them that we'd have any luck, but look at them now."

"They're beautiful, Grandmother," Caitlin agreed, reaching out to touch one of the blossoms.

"No, don't touch," her grandmother reprimanded her. "It might brown the flower."

"Sorry," Caitlin said quickly. "By the way, Grandmother, our senior class picnic is coming up, and I've been asked to select the site. Do you think we can use some of Ryan Mining's land?"

Regina Ryan looked at her granddaughter curiously. "Where did you have in mind?"

"I thought that tract right over the border in West Virginia."

Mrs. Ryan snorted. "I don't know why you'd want to go there."

"Does that mean we can't?" Caitlin asked. She should have known better than to think her grandmother would agree to anything she wanted.

But her grandmother's reply surprised her. "No, it's fine with me," Regina Ryan said almost absently. "We haven't mined there in years. If you want it, it's all yours."

"Oh, thanks!" Caitlin smiled with relief. She was just about to show her appreciation by giving her grandmother a hug, but the gesture was cut off by the maid's arrival with the dinner tray.

"Time for dinner, girls," Mrs. Ryan said, leading them to the sitting room.

They took their places at the round table in the middle of the room. Gold-rimmed Ainsley china had been set on top of a pale gold Irish linen tablecloth.

Quickly Catherine, the maid, served them their soup, a chilled seafood bisque. After Mrs. Ryan had sampled it, she nodded to the maid. "Excellent. Give Mrs. Crowley my compliments."

Catherine smiled and headed back to the kitchen. Mrs. Crowley was the longtime cook at Ryan Acres, and Caitlin considered her the best in Virginia.

"So, Caitlin," her grandmother said as she gracefully set down her soupspoon. "As I said, I looked over your college brochures. Some of the schools you are considering just are not worthy of your grades and background. I also noticed you hadn't included a Radcliffe brochure."

Caitlin cast a surreptitious glance toward Ginny.

"My alma mater, as you know," Regina Ryan continued. "I suppose I could understand if you were considering another Ivy League school, but the ones you've chosen just won't do at all. The business programs at several of these colleges are not the most comprehensive."

Caitlin raised another eyebrow toward Ginny. Since Mrs. Ryan was concentrating on her soup, she didn't notice. "I chose the schools I was most interested in," she said in her defense.

"You weren't thinking, Caitlin. These schools can't prepare you for what lies ahead. Your mother didn't have your academic talents, but she knew enough to choose a school that would prepare her for the eventual responsibility of overseeing Ryan Mining."

Caitlin drew up her courage and suddenly burst out, "But I don't want to concentrate only on business. I have a lot of interests, Grandmother. I want to go to a college that offers a lot of different courses."

Mrs. Ryan glanced up at her sharply. "You're not being realistic, Caitlin."

"Yes, I am. I don't think I'd make a good businesswoman."

"You're too young to know that," Regina Ryan said coolly.

"I may not know exactly what I want to do with my life. But I do know one thing. I don't want to run Ryan Mining."

"Nonsense." Regina Ryan scoffed at the idea. "You've known since you were a child that you'd be taking over the company someday."

"No, you're the one who's decided what my future should be. But it's *my* life, Grandmother. I ought to decide what I do with it."

"Enough!" Regina Ryan glared at her granddaughter. "This is not proper dinner table conversation. We'll discuss this later."

"Uh, I'm looking for the same kind of school as Caitlin, Mrs. Ryan," Ginny suddenly spoke up. "The school I go to will have to have riding facilities and good courses in management and agriculture, since I want to run a breeding farm someday. Radcliffe wouldn't be for me, or Barnard, for that matter—that's my mother's alma mater."

"Yes, of course. I see your point, but Caitlin is grooming herself to take over a huge mining concern. That should be her primary consideration in selecting a college."

Caitlin burst out sarcastically, "I could always try Brown."

Mrs. Ryan paused with her silver spoon balanced a half inch away from her soup plate. Her brow furrowed momentarily in thought. "You're quite right. That's an excellent idea," she said, deadly serious. "Yes, why didn't I think of that myself? I believe they have a good business program. I should be delighted to say that my granddaughter was attending Brown." She nodded as she dipped her spoon back into the soup. "Do get an application form."

Caitlin gave Ginny a desperate sidelong look under her lashes. Clearing her throat, she set her own soupspoon down on her plate. Brown. Now that her grandmother had the idea, she wasn't likely to let it go. Caitlin had only mentioned it because she was so angry. She had no idea whether she'd like to go there or not.

"Yes, Brown," Regina Ryan repeated as Catherine brought their main course. "Why didn't I think of it before?"

As the girls climbed the stairs to their bedroom an hour later, Ginny burst out before Caitlin had a chance to say a word. "I wish I could have helped you more in there."

"I know, but it's not your problem, Ginny. Sure, I'll inherit the mines, but I'd hire someone else to manage them. My grandmother can't see that, though. She can only see what *she* wants."

"Can't you reason with her?"

"Reason with my grandmother?" Caitlin said in amazement. "You saw how she acted at the table. If I keep pushing it, she'll just get cold and nasty and make sure I do exactly what she wants anyway."

"We'll think of something," Ginny said optimistically. "What's that saying—you can lead a horse to water, but you can't make it drink?

Caitlin started laughing. "I'll keep that in mind."

Ginny grinned. "You know, Brown isn't so bad. I wouldn't mind going there myself, except that it's in the middle of a city, and I couldn't stable Cinnamon easily."

"You're impossible, Ginny," Caitlin cried as they entered the bedroom.

"I know. That's why we get along so well."

As Caitlin settled into her bed she concluded that Brown might not be such a bad idea after all. It was in Rhode Island, several hundred miles away. She'd welcome the distance from her grandmother and her bossy ways. She needed to get away.

8

Early the next morning Caitlin and Ginny went riding, trying some of the fences Jeff had set up in preparation for hunt season. Both felt exhilarated as they walked up to the house from the stables and saw Regina Ryan, Laurence, and his parents waiting for them on the back terrace.

Mrs. Ryan was smiling as Caitlin and Ginny greeted the group. "Just in time, girls. The Baxters arrived five minutes ago," she said happily.

Laurence came forward and gave Caitlin a quick hug. "Been practicing, huh?" he asked.

"There's no such thing as enough where Appleveil is concerned." Caitlin grinned at him before turning to his parents. "Hello, Mr. and Mrs. Baxter," she said cordially. "It's nice to see you again. I'm so glad you've come this week-end."

"It's good to see you, too, Caitlin," Mr. Baxter replied.

"And we're certainly looking forward to riding this afternoon," Laurence's mother added.

"Mr. and Mrs. Baxter," Caitlin quickly broke in, "this is my friend, Ginny Brookes."

"How do you do, Ginny?" both Baxters said simultaneously. "You're a student at Highgate?" Mrs. Baxter added.

Ginny nodded. "Nice to meet you, too."

Regina Ryan interrupted, "I think if we are going to ride by one, we should sit down to lunch now." She motioned to the whole group. "Please come inside."

An hour and a half later they were all on horseback. "There's a good course through the woods," Mrs. Ryan announced. "Shall I lead?"

Without waiting for nods from her guests, she proceeded, and for the next two hours they followed her around the course. Ginny rode with Mrs. Ryan, the Baxters followed, and Caitlin and Laurence took up the rear; they were talking so much that their pace often slowed.

When they reached the open meadows again, where there were some magnificent fences dividing the pastures, Laurence and Caitlin drew up with the others. Her grandmother spoke briefly to the Baxters, explaining the course ahead. Caitlin, Laurence, and Ginny already knew it—a series of stone and split-rail fences separating pastures where horses were grazing; two streams, one shallow enough to ford, and a grand double oxer at the end. The last fence was the only manufactured one; the rest were part of the grounds.

Regina Ryan brought her mount around, circled the pasture at a canter, and approached the first fence, a stone wall. She was over and away, in a graceful move perfected by years of riding, and the others quickly followed. Ginny was handling Apris beautifully, Caitlin noticed, putting the mare over fences she'd never jumped, since she'd been schooled in the ring. The senior Baxters followed suit, but Caitlin wanted to try something different.

"I've got an idea, Laurence," she called, indicating he should pull his horse next to hers. "Let's jump over together."

"Sure," he said, smiling. "Shall we hold hands, too?"

"That may be going a little too far," Caitlin said.

They laughed to each other as Caitlin's mount, Challenger, and Devil Wind, whom Laurence rode when at Ryan Acres, lifted off the ground in the same stride, soared, and landed in tandem.

They continued to jump together, enjoying the challenge and the closeness, until they completed the full circle back to the Ryan Acres stable.

"Jeff," Regina Ryan called as the stable hand came running. "We'll walk them a bit and cool them out ourselves."

"Very well, Mrs. Ryan."

When the horses were cooled, Jeff and one of the other stable hands led them off into the stable, and the party of riders went up to the house. As they drifted through the french doors that led from the terrace to the rest of the house, Mrs. Ryan nodded at Caitlin. "Dinner will be at eight. Enjoy yourselves until then."

Caitlin turned to Laurence and Ginny. "Well, there's the swimming pool, and of course pool, darts, and the VCR in the game room. What do you want to do?"

"Frankly, I just want a hot bath," Ginny said. "Or maybe a cold one," she added, fanning her face. "I'll see you later."

"How about a swim?" Laurence asked Caitlin. "I'm warm enough for one."

"Sure. I'll run up and get my suit on. Meet me at the pool."

Quickly Caitlin followed Ginny up the stairs to her bedroom. As Caitlin went into the dressing room for her swimsuit, Ginny sat on the edge of the bed and began pulling off her boots.

"Your grandmother and I were talking while we were riding," Ginny said to Caitlin. "She really likes Laurence, you know."

"I know. She makes a point of telling me every time I mention his name."

"She said something about Jed, too."

Caitlin froze. "She did?"

"Not much, only that she was glad you weren't seeing him anymore. She thought he was 'charming'—to use her word—but that he didn't fit in with her plans for you."

"She came right out and said *her* plans for me?" Caitlin exclaimed, though it was not unusual for her grandmother to be so obvious.

"Pretty much, though I don't think she realized how it sounded. Anyway, it bothered her that Jed was from Montana. But she was really put off by his viewpoint on the mines. I guess he'd said something to her about restoring the land when she was finished mining it, filling in the old tunnels and planting trees and stuff."

"Well, I think she should, too."

"Does she know that?"

"I've mentioned it once or twice," Caitlin said sheepishly. "But I've never really pursued it. You know how angry she gets if I criticize anything having to do with Ryan Mining."

"Well, I guess Jed wasn't afraid."

"You'd think she'd respect him for that," Caitlin mused.

"That's the funny thing. She says she does. He just isn't what she wants for you."

Caitlin undressed and pulled on her bathing suit. "It doesn't matter now, anyway," she said sadly. "Jed hasn't changed his mind. He won't even talk to me." She thrust her arms into her terrycloth robe and grabbed a thick towel she had laid down on the bed. "I'd better go. Laurence is meeting me at the pool."

When Caitlin reached the pool, she pushed everything out of her mind. She wouldn't think about Jed, she told herself, as she dove like an arrow into the clear water. But as she surfaced, she realized it was easier said than done. No matter how hard she tried to push him away, Jed was never far from her thoughts.

Knowing how particular her grandmother could be, especially with guests, Caitlin dressed carefully for dinner in an elegant but simple blue silk dress.

"Do I look all right?" she asked Ginny before they left the room.

"You look great, as usual. I don't know what you're worried about. Your grandmother's not going to complain about that dress, and Laurence will love it."

They met the others in the formal living room at the front of the house. Margaret handed each of them a glass of Perrier as they entered.

Although Regina Ryan looked over with a smile and a nod, she continued chatting with the Baxters.

Laurence, handsome in a navy blazer and gray slacks, came hurrying over as soon as he spotted them.

"You look terrific." He smiled appreciatively at Caitlin, his pleasure at seeing her again written clearly on his face. "You, too, Ginny," he added.

"Looks like the old folks are having a good time," Ginny observed.

"You're not kidding. They haven't stopped talking. Before it was business. Now they're comparing notes on Europe," Laurence said.

The topic of the Baxters' and her grandmother's compatibility made Caitlin quite uncomfortable. Quickly she changed the subject. "I thought after dinner we could watch a tape."

"Sure. That sounds good to me," Laurence said.

At that moment Regina Ryan and the Baxters walked over. "Are you all ready to eat?" she asked cheerfully. "It's time to go in. My, you do look handsome tonight, Laurence."

"Thank you, Mrs. Ryan."

Their dinner conversation was comfortable, covering subjects they all enjoyed, yet Caitlin couldn't help noticing the special interest her grandmother was taking in Laurence.

"I understand you're quite the scholar, Laurence," she said to him midway through the meal. "What are your plans after graduation?"

"Well, I've thought of engineering or a career in the computer field."

"Wise choices. What schools are you considering?"

"M.I.T. looks good, but I've got some others in mind, too. Maybe Princeton."

"Not Brown?"

Caitlin nearly choked on the piece of roast beef she was chewing. She'd told Laurence that afternoon about the conversation she'd had with her grandmother.

"That's a possibility, too." Laurence smiled and cast a teasing glance at Caitlin.

Regina Ryan didn't notice. She'd turned to the Baxters. "I must say I've been proud of Caitlin's performance at Highgate. It's reassuring to know she'll be ready to take over Ryan Mining when I retire."

No! Caitlin screamed silently, but she knew what her grandmother's anger would be like if she voiced her protest aloud. Instead, she stared down at her plate, her eyes flashing with suppressed and frustrated fury. She was too well bred to speak out and contradict her grandmother just then.

But she wished she weren't. She wished she could tell her grandmother off once and for all.

9

Monday was a beautiful fall day. The clear sky was punctuated by a handful of cotton-puff clouds, and the air was crisp and sweet with the fragrance of the autumn plantings around the campus. Caitlin decided to vary her routine with Ian and take him out for a walk. "Not too far," she told him. "But I think a change of scenery's just what you need."

"Take me to see Duster!" Ian exclaimed.

Caitlin smiled. "I wish I could, but I'd have an awful time trying to get your wheelchair down the hill and back up again." Caitlin knew perfectly well that she could have carried Ian down to the stables, but she didn't want to make it too easy for him. She wanted to give him an incentive to walk again by pointing out the

98

disadvantages of being confined to a wheelchair. "We'll just take a walk around here today."

"Please, Caitlin—please." Ian turned around to look up at her with his big blue eyes.

She couldn't harden her heart against that pleading expression, as much as she knew she should. Ian had been able to do and see so little since his accident.

"All right," she said, finally relenting. "I'll carry you down. But afterward you're going to have to work extra hard on your exercises."

"I will," Ian said eagerly.

Caitlin found a spot near the top of the hill where she could park the wheelchair. Then she lifted Ian. Slowly, with the boy in her arms, she descended the brick stairway and crossed the grass toward the stable. She didn't notice as the tall boy leaving the soccer field paused to watch her progress.

Jed's curiosity got the better of him, and he watched as the two of them entered the stables. What was Caitlin up to? he wondered.

Inside the stables, Caitlin sat Ian on the bench outside Duster's stall. "Whew!" She let out a breath as she stood up. "You're heavier than I thought."

Ian giggled. "Which one is Duster?"

"Right here in this stall." She pointed. "I'll bring him out now."

"What are you doing here, Caitlin?" Jessica called from the aisle. "I thought you baby-sat in the afternoons."

Caitlin turned toward her friend. "I brought Ian down here to meet Duster."

Jessica smiled at Ian. "You going to take a ride?"

Caitlin hadn't thought that far ahead. "That's a great idea, Jessica. Would you like that, Ian?"

Ian looked dumbfounded at the suggestion. "But I can't—" he began.

Caitlin cut him off and gave him a reassuring smile. "It wouldn't be harder than sitting in your wheelchair. And I'll be right here with you. Why don't we tack up Duster and walk him around the paddock."

Ian seemed a little less frightened, his trust of Caitlin showing in his eyes.

"I'll get your tack," Jessica offered, "while you take Duster out."

"Thanks a lot, Jessica," Caitlin said as she reached for the stall door latch. "Hey, there, fella." She spoke softly to the horse. "How about a little ride? I have a friend I want you to meet."

Duster nickered and rubbed his muzzle against her arm. Carefully she brought him out of the stall and put him in his crossties.

"What do you think, Ian?" she asked.

"He's nice, but a lot bigger than I thought he'd be."

Jessica returned with the saddle and bridle.

"Now watch what I do, so you can remember how to do it yourself someday," Caitlin instructed. She hoisted the saddle onto Duster's back, settling it in precisely the right spot. Then she reached under Duster's belly for the girth strap. "I'm tightening it enough to keep it in place," she explained. "Then when I'm in the saddle I'll tighten it even more so there's no chance of it slipping."

"Am I really supposed to remember this?" Ian asked. "It sounds so complicated."

Caitlin laughed. "It really isn't, but I've been doing it so long it's second nature to me. Anyway, now I'm putting on the bridle." She threw the reins over Duster's head, then released the crossties, unbuckled his bridle, and slid it over his head, pressing the bit to his teeth. After he accepted it, she finished putting the bridle over his ears and secured the chin strap. "All set," she said when she was done.

"Doesn't it hurt him to have that metal in his mouth?" Ian questioned.

"Not with this bit." She walked Duster forward and pulled back his lips so Ian could see into his mouth. "The bit falls into this space right between his teeth. Would you like to pet him now?"

"I—I guess," Ian said nervously.

Caitlin drew Duster's head within the boy's reach. "Just pat his nose and tell him what a good boy he is."

Hesitantly Ian did as she instructed. "Good boy, Duster."

Duster nickered. "See, he likes you," Caitlin said. "I'm going to take him out in the paddock and tighten his girth. Then I'll be right back for you."

Out in the bright sunshine, Caitlin mounted quickly and reached down to tighten the girth. Then she tested the stirrups to make sure the buckles were secure. Satisfied, she dismounted and tied Duster to the fence. Then she went back inside for Ian.

Jed had been ready to leave when he saw Caitlin reappear in the paddock, leading Duster. His eyes widened in amazement when she came out of the stable a minute later with Ian and lifted him into the saddle. After untying Duster, Caitlin vaulted into the saddle behind Ian. Jed was close enough to hear her words clearly as she spoke calmly and encouragingly to the boy.

"After you get used to the feel of this, I'll let you ride alone while I lead Duster around," she said.

Caitlin wouldn't have taken the risk with Ian if Duster had been a less mild-mannered animal. But she knew he wouldn't object to the extra weight of the boy, as some horses might have. Caitlin continued to talk comfortingly to both Duster and Ian as they walked around the paddock. "Grab his mane," she told Ian. "It won't hurt him. That's it. Hold tightly." Gently she maneuvered Ian's legs so he sat astride and kept one arm fixed steadily on his waist.

Duster did a few prancing steps, but Caitlin quickly calmed him. She began to feel Ian's tense body relax a little. "It's not so scary, is it?" she asked him.

"No, it's fun," Ian said. "Could we go faster?"

"Hey, not so fast, Ian. Let's take it one step at a time."

Jed was mystified. Caitlin's behavior with Ian didn't fit in with his expectations. He'd come to the conclusion that her work with Ian had been motivated purely by guilt and not by any real concern for the boy. But her actions were proving him wrong. She really appeared to care about Ian. Jed saw how patiently she helped Ian over his fear. More importantly, Ian's trust and adoration of Caitlin were clearly evident.

Jed knew he shouldn't be spying like that, but he felt compelled to stay and watch.

Caitlin

"Do your legs hurt?" Caitlin asked Ian after they'd walked around the ring a few times.

"A little, but it's okay." Ian was so filled with excitement over his new adventure that he wasn't afraid any longer.

"Now it's time for you to try it yourself. I'll walk with you, but first I've got to shorten the stirrups." After she tied Duster to the fence, she raised the right stirrup. She measured it against Ian's dangling leg to make sure it was the right length. Satisfied, she then bent Ian's leg slightly and put his foot in the iron. She couldn't help noticing the brief grimace of pain on his face, but for once he didn't cry out. She repeated the same steps with the left stirrup.

"Hold the mane tightly," she instructed.

Carefully she led Duster around the ring, walking to the side of his head so she could get to Ian quickly if he needed her. But the boy was doing well on his own, enjoying the ride so much that he couldn't stop smiling.

"Can you push your feet into the stirrups, Ian?"

"I don't know," he replied.

"Try."

Caitlin could see him make an effort. "It hurts. My legs feel funny," he told her.

"You're doing fine, Ian. We'll take it a little at a time."

104

True Love

Caitlin was pleased by the expression of concentration on Ian's face that indicated he was trying. The voluntary effort was much more than he usually made in his regular exercises. *Maybe riding is the answer,* she thought excitedly.

"I'm so proud of you, Ian. Would you like to come back and ride again tomorrow?"

"Yes!" he cried.

"Okay." Caitlin patted his leg, then reached up to lift him from the saddle.

Jed turned away then and headed through the cluster of trees back to his dorm. He wanted to wipe the image of Caitlin he'd just witnessed from his mind. He didn't feel she deserved his positive thoughts after what she'd done. He didn't even know why he'd wasted his time by watching her. She was no concern of his anymore. She'd lied to him, she'd hurt Diana, and she didn't even have enough courage to admit her guilt to the Fosters.

Yet as soon as he returned to his room, Jed felt compelled to reread the letter he'd received from Diana the previous day. He'd been so happy to hear how much she loved her new school and how she'd already made several new friends. But he'd been disturbed by her frequent mentions of how Caitlin had helped her recover. Diana had written:

Please give her another chance. I was really upset when you wrote to tell me how you'd told her off. Sure, Caitlin was wrong in letting me take the blame, but that's all in the past. She's suffering for what she did, Jed, and I've forgiven her. Look at what she's done to try to make up for her mistake. If it wasn't for her, I'd probably still be in the hospital now—or maybe even dead. And she really cares about Ian, even if you don't think so.

Jed held the letter in his hand as he stared out his window at a group of boys playing Frisbee in the late-afternoon sun. Part of him felt Diana was right, that he'd let Caitlin suffer enough for her misdeed. But there was another part of him that felt she could never be punished enough for having ruined so many lives. And that part prevented him from making any overtures of forgiveness.

10

Thursday night after dinner Caitlin drove to the shopping center near Martinsville. She needed a couple of new notebooks and some shampoo, but the main purpose of her trip was to get off campus for an hour or so.

She parked outside one of the department stores and went in through the revolving doors. Going immediately to the stationery department, she selected three notebooks, then she headed across the store toward the toiletries. On her way she passed the jewelry counter and couldn't resist pausing to look at the selection of earrings on tall, revolving racks. Caitlin had large quantities of good jewelry, but she loved fun, inexpensive earrings.

Slowly she turned the rack, pulling off a couple of pairs and holding them up one at a time to her ears and examining herself in the small mirror glued to the rack. As she held up a pair of dangling red earrings, she happened to glance across to the main jewelry counter where the better-quality items were kept. What she saw made her gasp.

Her father was standing at the far side of the counter, and at his side was an attractive, blond-haired woman. Despite herself, Caitlin couldn't draw her eyes away from the two of them. The woman was in her thirties, well dressed in a lightweight knit suit, and clearly enjoying the company of Gordon Westlake. Dr. Westlake grinned at something the woman said and laid a hand on her arm. Then he looked across the display counter—right into Caitlin's appraising eyes.

Caitlin averted her gaze back to the earrings, hoping the two of them would go away and leave her alone. But a moment later Dr. Westlake was by her side, one arm leaning against the counter directly in front of her. "Hello, Caitlin. It's good to see you again."

Caitlin didn't answer. Ignoring him, she pulled a pair of blue enamel earrings off the rack and held them near her ear.

"They're pretty," her father told her. "But I think the red ones would look even nicer on you."

Caitlin threw the earrings down on the counter. "How would you know?" she spat out.

"Just a guess," he said, shrugging. He turned to the woman, who had come over, too. "Caitlin, I'd like you to meet a friend of mine, Marcia Chambers. She works with me at the hospital." He grinned. "Actually, she practically runs the place. I'd be lost without her." He clasped Marcia's hand warmly. "Marcia, this is Caitlin."

For a moment Caitlin was confused. This was a side of Gordon Westlake she'd never seen before—a caring, affectionate side she'd refused to believe was genuine.

"Nice to meet you," Caitlin said politely, though tension was evident in her voice.

The older woman extended a hand, which Caitlin took reluctantly. "It's nice to meet you. Your father has told me a lot about you."

Caitlin's eyes bore down on Dr. Westlake, her momentary warming toward him now gone. "You have no right to say you're my father."

"But I am," he replied. "You can't deny the truth. I want to keep in touch with you. I was hoping that you'd answer my letters or return my phone calls."

"Why should I?" she said through clenched teeth. "You don't mean anything to me. You think you can ignore me for almost seventeen years and then suddenly come back and play father?"

"I never meant to leave you alone. I told you that. But I can understand why you wouldn't want to believe me. I suspect your grandmother told you enough lies to poison you against me."

"My grandmother is not a liar," Caitlin said, trying to keep her voice even. "Now, if you'll excuse me, I've got to get back to school." Caitlin started to step away from the counter, but Dr. Westlake held her back.

"Go if you have to," he said. "I just want to tell you one thing. No matter what your grandmother may have told you, I loved your mother very much. We could have been so happy together. If only—"

Caitlin cut him off. "I don't want to hear any more of your lies. Now leave me alone. And don't bother my friends anymore, either." Earlier that week she'd received a letter from Diana indicating that he'd asked her if she'd heard from Caitlin.

"You mean Diana?" he asked. "I admit it may have been improper to write to her, but I did it only because I hadn't heard from you."

"Well, you'd better get used to it. As far as I'm concerned, you don't exist." Shaking off his grasp, she turned around and ran out of the store, leaving everything she had planned to buy on the counter.

As she hurried to her car, she thought about going back and telling him that if he didn't leave her alone she'd have her grandmother take legal action against him. But she thought better of it. She'd already given him more of her time than he deserved.

It rained the following afternoon, so Caitlin was unable to take Ian down to the stables. Instead, they worked on Ian's exercises indoors and picked up their board game where they'd left off a few days earlier.

"This isn't as much fun as riding Duster," Ian complained.

"I know, Ian, but we can't go riding in this weather."

"Can we go tomorrow?"

"Tomorrow's Saturday, but we can go on Monday if it's nice out and the paddock's not too muddy."

Ian was quiet for a moment, then said, "I guess I don't mind playing this game, either."

"Well, I like it," Caitlin said, trying to cheer him up. "And I like you."

"I like you, too, Caitlin. You're a lot more fun than my old baby-sitter. She used to make me play by myself because she was always reading books and things."

"She was doing her homework." Caitlin felt compelled to speak up on Diana's behalf. "Besides, you weren't sick then." She wished she could have taken the words back as soon as they were out of her mouth.

Ian nodded, then said with childish simplicity, "But it was her fault I got hurt."

"No, Ian! You shouldn't say that. It's not true!"

"Yes, it is," Ian insisted. "When I got sick and called her, she didn't come. Then I fell down."

"Ian, please, don't think that way about Diana!"

He looked at Caitlin innocently. "Why?"

As he asked the question, every bit of Caitlin's guilt rushed to the surface, threatening to overwhelm her. She couldn't stand it anymore! Even this sweet little boy was blaming Diana, a girl who'd done nothing. Something inside Caitlin cracked. She couldn't keep the truth to herself any longer. She couldn't allow Diana to continue to be blamed!

Caitlin knelt before Ian's wheelchair and took his hands. "Diana didn't do anything wrong. She's a sweet and wonderful person, and it wasn't her fault that you got sick."

"I heard my mom and dad talking. They said she wasn't watching me. It was her fault I got hurt. She didn't stop me from going into that shed and eating the stuff that made me sick. She could have. That's what a baby-sitter's for, isn't it?"

"Ian," Caitlin pleaded, "she didn't tell you not

to go in the shed because she thought it was locked. She locked it herself!"

"It wasn't locked. It was open."

"Because I'd been there to get something. I was in a hurry and forgot to lock the door again."

Ian stared at her wide-eyed. "It was your fault?" he asked disbelievingly.

"Ian, I'm sorry! I didn't mean to keep it a secret. I didn't mean for Diana to be blamed. I didn't even know what happened or know that you'd gone into the shed until much, much later."

"But I thought you were my friend!" Ian cried.

"I *am* your friend!"

Tears were streaming down Ian's cheeks, and his mouth was puckered. "No, you're not. I don't like you anymore, Caitlin. You're bad."

"Ian, I'm sorry I didn't tell you. But I was so afraid you'd be upset."

Ian had pulled his hands out of her grasp and turned his head away from her. "Go away!" he said, sobbing. "I hate you! I never want to see you again."

"I can't leave you alone, Ian. I've got to stay until your mother comes home. Please believe me. I'm sorry for what I did—really sorry! Can't you forgive me, Ian?"

He wouldn't answer. His cheeks were still wet with tears, but his face was pouting and stony.

"We were doing so well," Caitlin pleaded. "Your legs are getting stronger. Pretty soon you'll be able to ride Duster by yourself—and walk again!"

"I'll *never* walk—not ever! I don't want you to baby-sit for me anymore, either!"

"No, no, Ian. Just because you're mad at me, don't say you won't walk again. You will!" Caitlin was crying herself by then. This couldn't be happening. Ian couldn't be turning against her, too.

But the little boy's expression was stubborn and withdrawn. "Go away! I don't want to see you anymore!" He wouldn't look at her, and when she tried to make him respond, he turned the other way.

Caitlin tried to dry her own tears. Soon Mrs. Foster would be home. She had to think quickly. What was she going to do?

"Please, Ian," she begged one last time before his mother arrived. "I'm so sorry. It was an accident. Can't we be friends again?"

He wouldn't answer her. He did nothing but sit unmoving in his wheelchair, staring across the room. "All right, be mad at me," she cried. "But please don't just sit there and stare."

He remained unresponsive, as if he hadn't heard her. Desperate, Caitlin brought him a glass of milk and cookies. He pushed them away.

Caitlin felt as if she wanted to die. Like it or not, she'd have to tell the Fosters the truth now. She'd start from the beginning and explain everything. She couldn't expect a seven-year-old to understand what had been going through her head all this time. But Mrs. Foster had always struck her as being kind and sensitive. Caitlin prayed she'd understand.

But she wasn't ready when she heard the front door open and Elaine Foster's footsteps in the hall. "Hello. I'm home," she called out.

Caitlin rushed to meet Mrs. Foster before she came into the family room and saw her scowling son.

"Hi," Caitlin said, forcing a smile.

"Hi, Caitlin." Elaine Foster smiled as Caitlin stepped through the doorway into the hall. "Where's Ian?"

"In there." Caitlin indicated the family room. Mrs. Foster began to move in that direction, but Caitlin blocked her way.

"What's going on?" Mrs. Foster asked suspiciously.

The time had come to tell the Fosters the truth. Caitlin would have to take the chance of facing more rejection or having more anger directed against her. She had no choice. If she didn't tell the Fosters now, she knew Ian would.

"Can I talk to you for a minute, Mrs. Foster?" Caitlin said quickly. "In the kitchen?"

Elaine Foster frowned. "Is something wrong?"

"Well," Caitlin continued as the older woman followed her into the kitchen, out of Ian's earshot, "I've got something to tell you. I know I should have told you sooner, but I was afraid."

Mrs. Foster reached across the kitchen table where they'd sat down and patted Caitlin's hands. "I'm your friend. You can tell me."

Caitlin couldn't look Mrs. Foster in the eye. Instead she pulled her hand away and stared down at the linoleum floor. "I have a confession to make. It goes back to the day of Ian's accident. I've let you believe all this time that Diana was careless and left the shed unlocked." Caitlin swallowed as she wasted no time getting to the point. "She didn't. I did."

Elaine Foster frowned in puzzlement. "It was you?" As the realization began to sink in, Caitlin could see the revulsion begin to cloud Mrs. Foster's face.

"Please, you've got to let me explain," Caitlin pleaded.

Elaine Foster slumped deeper into her chair. "I don't believe it. You've been so kind to him," she said almost in a state of shock.

"It was an accident—an awful, tragic accident," Caitlin said. "I came to get a prop for the fund-raiser. We needed a pitchfork. I unlocked the shed and found the pitchfork, but I was in such a hurry when I left that I forgot to lock the door again. I saw Ian out in the yard playing, but he didn't see me. It never occurred to me that I'd done anything wrong until the report of Ian's accident appeared in the newspaper. Then I realized that I was the one responsible.

"I was so scared and upset, I didn't know what to do. I took my horse out riding in the rain and got sick and spent a week in bed. When I got better, I still didn't say anything. It was awful of me, I know, but three weeks had already gone by. I thought if I just forgot it, it would all go away."

"So you let Diana take the blame," Mrs. Foster noted. "Oh, what that poor girl went through. I said such terrible things to her."

"I didn't know that at the time," Caitlin went on. "I thought since Diana went away I could just let you think it was her fault. But then I felt so guilty and terrible, I wanted to try to make up for what I'd done. I wanted to help Ian get well again. I *had* to. Then over the summer I found out that Diana had anorexia nervosa—caused by everything she'd been through. I had no idea how much she was suffering. I had to help her, so I went to the hospital where she was a patient and volunteered. She was in bad shape, but I worked with her for days, then finally, when I told her Ian's accident wasn't her fault she started to respond.

"It took nearly all summer for her to recover,

but she's fine now. She's going to a new school in Pennsylvania and doing really well."

"Why didn't you tell us sooner?" Mrs. Foster asked. "How could you deceive us like this?"

"I was afraid, and when Diana told me she didn't mind your still blaming her, I used that as an excuse."

"I'm going to have to call her and tell her how sorry we are—about everything. She should know we know the truth."

"Yes," Caitlin agreed. "Today Ian said something about Diana not taking care of him the way she should have, and I knew I couldn't let him go on thinking that she was to blame. I told him the truth." Caitlin shook her head sadly. "He didn't take it very well. He told me he doesn't want me to take care of him anymore. He says he hates me."

Caitlin suddenly burst into tears. "I'm so sorry, Mrs. Foster. I did such a terrible thing by not telling everyone the truth right at the start."

Elaine Foster suddenly rose, walked around the table, and put her arm around Caitlin's shoulders. "You were wrong, Caitlin, and I won't say that I'm not shocked by what you've just told me. But I can understand why it's been so difficult for you to admit the truth."

"You can?"

"If you hadn't tried to make up for it by helping Diana and Ian, I probably wouldn't be so understanding. But, somehow, I think you've paid the price for not telling the truth. You've had to live with your guilt."

"It's been terrible!"

"At least you've confessed to Diana and cleared her conscience. If nothing else, I think you've learned a lesson from this, Caitlin."

Caitlin nodded numbly. "I'll never let anyone else suffer for something I've done again. But Ian hates me now. I've hurt him again!"

"I'll talk to Ian and try to explain to him what it cost you to tell him the truth. I think he'll come around. But, for now, it would be better if you didn't sit for him."

Caitlin felt her heart breaking, but she knew Mrs. Foster was right. "Try to make him understand, Mrs. Foster. I care about him so much. Tell him how very, very sorry I am."

"I will."

Caitlin sniffed back a sob. "I guess I'd better go. I'll get my things and say good-bye to Ian."

Elaine Foster followed Caitlin into the family room. Ian still sat there, his face set in an angry, withdrawn scowl.

Caitlin knelt down quickly beside him. "Ian, please don't hate me. I'm so sorry. I never meant to hurt you."

The little boy made no response.

"I'm going to go, but I'll always be your friend if you want me to," she told him.

When Ian still said nothing, Caitlin rose and walked across to where Elaine Foster was standing in the doorway. "I'm really sorry."

"I think you'd better go now."

Caitlin bit her lip to keep herself from bursting into tears again. "Good-bye, Mrs. Foster."

"Good-bye, Caitlin."

Although the rain had tapered off to a light mist, Caitlin pulled the hood of her slicker over her head as if she could hide beneath it. She felt better telling her secret, but it didn't come close to easing her pain for all the hurt she'd caused poor Ian. Her shoulders sagged, and she started to cry again.

When she got back to the dorm, Caitlin went into the bathroom and splashed cold water on her face to try to disguise her red eyes. But Ginny was too preoccupied with packing her things for the hunt to notice that Caitlin was upset.

"Do you think your grandmother minds having Bert and me overnight?" she asked, without looking up from her overnight case.

"No. I told you she offered," Caitlin said with uncharacteristic testiness.

"Just checking!" Ginny replied defensively.

Caitlin went to her dresser and removed a few articles, which she then dropped on the bed. She was glad her habit and white stock were clean and hanging in the closet. Her dress hunt boots were gleaming from the polish Rollins had given them on her last trip home. She pulled a large canvas bag from under the bed and stuffed the things inside carelessly.

"Why are you in such a bad mood?" Ginny asked, turning to watch Caitlin's haphazard packing.

"I told Ian and Mrs. Foster the truth."

Ginny rushed to Caitlin's side. "What happened? It must have been awfully rough," she said, trying to console her friend.

Caitlin nodded and sat down on the bed. "Mrs. Foster actually understood—which made me feel more ashamed than ever."

"Oh, you'll get over that," Ginny said encouragingly.

Caitlin brushed back another tear. "But Ian hates me now. He wouldn't talk to me. He doesn't want me to come over anymore." Restlessly Caitlin jumped up and went to the closet. She took out her riding habit and hung it on the back of the door.

"I can't believe he means it," Ginny said.

"He said he'd never walk again. Now, because of me, he's going to undo all the progress he's made."

"No, he won't, Caitlin. Kids never stay angry for long. But the important thing is, you've finally told the truth. You don't have to feel guilty anymore. Caitlin, you did the right thing. I'm proud of you."

Caitlin managed a weak smile. "Thanks, Ginny. I know I had to tell them, it's just that I feel it's too late. Jed won't forgive me, and Ian may not. I'll never be able to make up for what I did."

"Wait and see. It'll be okay."

"I hope you're right." Caitlin sighed, not sharing Ginny's optimism.

"You'll see," Ginny went on. "Now, if I were you, I'd start thinking about the hunt on Sunday and the race tomorrow. There's nothing like a good chase through the woods to get your mind off your troubles."

Despite herself, Caitlin smiled. "Ginny, if it were that simple, the whole world would be riding horses."

"Well, maybe it *is* that simple, Caitlin. Maybe it is."

11

The Ryans, the Baxters, Ginny, and Bert arrived at the Appleveil estate early Saturday morning. Quite a few horse vans were already drawn up on the parking field. Around and between them scurried an ever-growing crowd of habited riders leading their mounts, spectators dressed in street clothes, and van drivers and stable boys leading out and tacking up other horses.

An electric excitement was in the air. The previous day's rainstorm had left everything clear and sparkling. But Caitlin didn't feel the excitement. She'd thought getting away from Highgate and out with other people would be an answer, but she still felt depressed. Laurence had tried to cheer her up, knowing the reason for her sadness, and she made an effort to smile once in a while because she didn't want her grandmother asking if something was wrong.

"Let's find the vans," Regina Ryan called as they climbed out of her Bentley. Laurence's parents, grandparents, and a friend of theirs, William Oakes, got out of the Baxters' Jaguar sedan parked next to it. "Jeff should have parked them fairly close to the drive. I think I see them," Mrs. Ryan called a second later, striding ahead of the others. She cut an elegant figure in her dark blue riding habit and could have passed for a much younger woman. "Yes, there they are." She motioned the others to follow.

The Ryan and Baxter vans were parked side by side. Jeff and the Baxter driver already had the horses out and tacked up. Caitlin had wanted to ride Duster, so Jeff had driven over to Highgate to pick up Duster and Laurence's horse, Satellite.

The riding party led their horses away from the parking area to a field a short distance away, where the other riders were gathering. In the distance was the Appleveil manor house with its magnificently well-kept stables.

About sixty riders were gathered for the preliminary warm-up race. There would be more the following day for the hunt. The course had been marked out, but it was up to the individual riders to see and follow the markers. They

would go out in pairs, and those with the best
time over the course would be the winners.

As they lined up, waiting for their turns,
Laurence smiled at Caitlin. "Are you nervous?"
he asked.

"No." She shook her head, having ridden
hunt-chases many times before. "Should I be?"

"No, but you're so quiet. I hope the ride will
do you good."

Caitlin shrugged, and then the timer was
signaling Laurence and her to start off. They put
Duster and Satellite to a fast canter over the
field, watching as they came down the slope for
the first of the trail markers. Laurence spotted it.
"Over there!"

They headed the horses toward the low stone
wall and wooden trail indicated by the markers.
The fence was easy, and they soared over, one
behind the other.

The wooded trail led out into another small
meadow. There they had to slow and search for
the marker. Caitlin saw it first and noted it led
to another fence, with a second obstacle two
strides beyond it. The total length of the course
was three miles, so they had to pace the horses
carefully. Too much speed and the horses would
be blown out before the end of the course; not
enough, and they'd lag behind in their time.

The markers led them through water obstacles, up steep, rocky trails, and around a curve where an unexpected jump suddenly faced them. That was no problem for Caitlin, as Duster could jump from a standstill. She was pleased to see how well Laurence was handling Satellite, too.

The horses were exhilarated, snorting in excitement, and soon some of their excitement rubbed off on Caitlin. She began to forget her problems and started to think of the ride. She turned to Laurence and heard him laugh as they passed the team that had set out ahead of them. She gave him a thumbs-up sign as they galloped into an open meadow.

Then they approached the last mile of the course. It was the most difficult of all, truly testing both rider and animal. There were two fences facing each other at a ninety-degree angle. The horses had to land off one jump, immediately pivot, stride once, and jump again. Laurence and Caitlin flew through the sequence with little trouble. Then there was another water obstacle, a long gallop down a dirt lane, a rocky, wooden trail with two fences, and a canter to the finish line with one last four-foot brush. They crossed the finish line nose to nose as the timer's stopwatch clicked.

"Wow." Caitlin laughed as they slowed the

orses to walk them back to the starting line.
That was good practice for tomorrow."

"Yeah," Laurence said breathlessly. "But I
don't think the fox will give us such a hard
time."

"How do you think we did?"

"Well, it's hard to say until we see some of the
other riders' times."

Since they'd been the second-to-last pair to go
off, the others in the group were already gathered waiting for the annoucer to call out the
order of the finish times.

"How'd it go?" Ginny called to Caitlin.

"Well, I think. How about you?"

"Not bad. Cinnamon shied a little at the water,
but you know how he hates to get wet."

In a moment Regina Ryan and her partner,
William Oakes, and the Baxters rode over.

"Well." Mrs. Ryan smiled. "That was in-
vigorating, wasn't it?"

"Sure was," Laurence agreed.

"For myself, I'll be happy to be in the top
twenty," she remarked cheerfully. "What do you
think, William?"

"I think we did very well, Regina, considering
the competition we're up against."

The loudspeaker crackled a moment later.
"We have the final times," a voice echoed into
the afternoon air. "The best time, at seven

minutes thirty seconds, goes to number seventeen."

Everyone looked around quickly at the numbered white cards pinned to each rider's back. A moment later two women in their twenties gasped excitedly. The rest of the riders began to applaud.

"Second, in seven minutes thirty-eight seconds, to number twenty-five."

Ginny let out a whoop. "We did it, Bert! We did it!"

"Congratulations," the others began calling as Ginny and Bert were showered with applause.

The announcer continued running down a list of times and numbers in order of finish. Caitlin and Laurence finished eighth, just ahead of her grandmother and William Oakes. The Baxters finished fifteenth.

Caitlin was mildly disappointed that she hadn't finished higher. "I thought we'd done a lot better," she whispered to Laurence as they walked toward the car.

"So did I, but we were working with a handicap," he reminded her. "Because we were practically last, we had to trample through everyone else's mud. That must have slowed us down more than we thought. Besides, finishing eighth out of thirty pairs isn't so bad."

"You're right," she said, looking into his

sparkling eyes. She wiped all thoughts of horses from her mind as she concentrated on Laurence during the ride back to Ryan Acres.

But her grandmother thought of nothing but the morning's ride. During lunch she made a point of singling out Ginny. "You rode exceptionally well today. You ought to be proud of yourself."

"Coming from you, that's quite a compliment," Ginny said, her head bent modestly.

"Maybe you can give Caitlin a few pointers. She should have done better today," Mrs. Ryan added, directing her words at Ginny, not at Caitlin.

"There was nothing wrong with Caitlin's ride," Ginny said in her friend's defense.

But the damage had been done as far as Caitlin was concerned. It was just one more indication that she was a disappointment to her grandmother. Nothing Caitlin did was ever good enough for the perfection-seeking Regina Ryan. If Caitlin got a B in a course at Highgate, her grandmother wanted to know why it wasn't an A. If she helped raise two thousand dollars at a fund-raiser, her grandmother wondered why it wasn't three. Her choice of colleges was all wrong, and, with the exception of Laurence, so was her choice of boyfriends. Would she ever do anything right as far as Regina Ryan was concerned?

Caitlin could think of nothing else as she entertained her friends for the rest of the day. Her pleasant facade masked the rage that was boiling inside her. *I'll show her,* she kept telling herself. *Tomorrow I'm going to run a course that's going to make her sit up and take notice of me at last!*

Caitlin's dark mood was still with her when the bright sun awakened her the following morning. She smiled her way through a light breakfast, but her thoughts were on the hunt.

When she and the rest of the Ryan Acres party arrived at Appleveil, they saw other red-jacketed riders milling around on the gravel drive in front of the main house, sipping the cups of coffee and warmed cider that were being handed out by the staff. Despite the distance, Caitlin could hear the yapping and occasional braying of the foxhounds who sensed the excitement in the air. They were kept in the kennel behind the Georgian colonial manor house until the fox was released and the hunt ready to begin.

Laurence, Caitlin, Ginny, and Bert stood together as they sipped their cider, waving and saying hello to the many people they knew.

"You haven't ridden this hunt before, have you, Bert?" Caitlin asked. It was a struggle for her to engage in polite conversation when inwardly she seethed with rage and self-loathing, but she didn't want anyone to think there was anything wrong.

Bert shook his head. "My first fox hunt, but I figure to do all right as long as I stick right on Ginny's heels."

"Spoken like a true horseman," Ginny said, pleased by her boyfriend's compliment.

"At least the ground's not so sloppy as it was yesterday," she added. "I hate getting all that mud in my face."

"If you stay at the head of the pack, that won't be a problem," Laurence said.

At that moment they heard the sharp blast of the master of the hunt's long brass horn, signaling them to mount. The dogs, still on leashes, were being led from the kennels toward the bottom of the field.

"The fox is off," Ginny cried excitedly. "Good luck, everyone!"

"Good luck," Caitlin called as they raced for their horses. "See you at the kill," she yelled over her shoulder.

The dogs were soon released, and the chorus of their brays carried up the hill to where the hunt participants had gathered. The master of the hunt blew the signal that set the riders off, following the trail of the dogs.

Laurence and Caitlin stayed together as they pounded with the pack across the field, although Caitlin paid little attention to anyone's position but her own.

Laurence made no attempt to hold Caitlin back as she rode fearlessly and aggressively. They stayed near the head of the pack of riders as the hunt wove across the countryside like a bright red swarm of bees, the pack gradually unbunching as some riders lagged behind and others forged toward the lead.

On and on they rode over the glorious Virginia countryside. Caitlin thought of none of the dangers of the hunt as she headed Duster over the many fences breaking the fields and urged him up and down steep embankments as the fox took cover in the woods and the hounds followed. She was aware that Laurence was right behind her, but she didn't turn to look. Her concentration was solely on her riding. Down a steep incline they went, where a stone wall awaited them at the bottom. It was a dangerous jump, but Caitlin gathered Duster and flew over. She knew that not all the riders would take that fence, preferring instead to walk their horses along its length until they found an easier passage.

Soon she and Laurence came to the top of a grassy hill. Circling across the field below, Caitlin saw the hunt master and leaders closing in on the heels of the dogs. She realized the fox must be seeking a hole if the dogs were slowing. She also saw a shortcut that would take her to the pack in half the time. But it was a difficult route, involving several stone pasture fences and a plunge through a thick piece of woodland where almost anything could happen. But Caitlin was determined to be there when the fox was cornered. Without a moment's hesitation, she headed Duster toward the short cut.

"No, Caitlin," Laurence suddenly called from behind her. "It's too dangerous!"

Caitlin pretended she didn't hear him as she urged Duster into the woods. Branches and brambles were constant obstacles in their way, but Caitlin deftly led Duster around them. They jumped over a tree that blocked their path and forded a narrow stream, and with an uncanny sense of direction, Caitlin heeled Duster forward into the small open pasture beyond the wood.

Swinging in a wide circle, Caitlin headed Duster toward the several large stone fences ahead of them. Timing his strides to perfection, she waited until exactly the right moment before squeezing her legs into his sides. Up and over they went, soaring like birds. It was a risky maneuver. All it would have taken was one false move, and Duster might have gone down on the rocks, where he would have certainly broken a leg. But Caitlin didn't allow herself to think of that possibility. There was one more high fence to clear, followed by a steep downhill grade, which would make for a difficult landing. Again, using all her equestrian skills, she got Duster over, pulling him up as they landed and collecting him for the downhill descent.

Once they were down the grade, they were closing in on the pack. A moment later Caitlin and Duster joined the surprised hunt master and four other riders, each of whom was a seasoned rider-to-the-hounds.

"He's holed up," the master cried, charging forward into the copse where the dogs circled and yowled. Caitlin was right with the other four riders as they charged into the copse to find the fox well protected in a deep pocket under the roots of an old oak. The trapped animal snarled and snapped at the hounds' noses every time they got too close.

The master blew a silent whistle, calling off the dogs. Well trained, the pack of hounds answered the whistle's command and moved away, still whimpering and looking longingly at their quarry.

Other riders began pounding up, including

Laurence, who rode immediately to Caitlin's side.

"Are you crazy?" he hissed, worry written all over his face. "You could have killed yourself, and Duster, too!"

Caitlin had begun to relax as if her hell-bent ride had succeeded in draining a terrible poison from her system.

She smiled and said breathlessly, "I made it, though, didn't I?"

"And I followed you," Laurence said, frowning, "so I know the chances you took. I didn't even try to put Satellite over that second fence. I took him around, but I saw you and Duster taking it!"

"I knew he could do it, Laurence," Caitlin said soothingly. "Duster and I made it. We're fine."

Laurence could only shake his head.

As the tired riders headed back to Appleveil at a more leisurely pace, Regina Ryan rode up to her granddaughter. She looked questioningly at Caitlin. "That was some mad ride you took," she said. "What got into you?"

"I wanted to get there first," Caitlin said.

"But you risked injuring Duster."

"No, I didn't," Caitlin said defiantly. "I know my horse, Grandmother, and I didn't make him do anything I didn't think he was capable of handling. Isn't that the point of these hunts—to test the limits of your horsemanship?"

Mrs. Ryan flashed her granddaughter a rare smile. "Well said, Caitlin. The results speak for themselves. You rode well, today."

"Thank you, Grandmother."

"Let's go up to the manor house for brunch," Mrs. Ryan said. "I can't wait to introduce you to my hunt friends. Everyone will be wanting to hear about your ride."

Caitlin beamed as she followed her grandmother to the Appleveil mansion. She couldn't have asked for anything more. Those few complimentary words from her grandmother more than made up for the hurt she'd suffered the day before.

12

The next day at Highgate Emily came over to Caitlin's table at lunch.

"Hi, Emily!" Caitlin called. "It's good to see you. Where have you been hiding yourself?" They'd hardly talked to each other since the night the girls had all gathered in Caitlin's room to plan the party.

"Mostly in the physics lab, I'm afraid," Emily said, adding, "I've been seeing a lot of Terry, too."

"I thought so." Caitlin winked.

Emily's cheeks flushed. "Listen," she added, "I need to talk to you. Can we get together sometime later today?"

"Sure," Caitlin answered, intrigued. Did Emily have some news about Jed? "How about this afternoon?" Caitlin suggested.

"Great, but I thought you were sitting for Ian."

Caitlin sighed. "I was until last Friday. I had to give it up. I couldn't keep up with everything." It was the wrong time to tell her what had really happened with Ian.

Emily nodded. "Diana used to complain about that, too. You can't do your homework and baby-sit at the same time." Emily shook her head as if trying to rid herself of bad memories, then looked at Caitlin. "This afternoon's fine with me. Your room or mine?"

"I have a better idea. Why don't I drive us into town, and we'll have a soda or something?"

"Great!" Emily exclaimed. "I'd love to get away for an afternoon."

"I'll meet you at three-thirty in the parking lot behind the dorm."

"I'll be there," Emily promised.

It took only fifteen minutes for the two girls to get to Martinsville, the closest town. Caitlin kept the conversation on Emily as they breezed down the country roads. She was genuinely glad to hear how happy her friend was with her boyfriend, Terry, and how much she was enjoying school that year.

In Martinsville Caitlin pulled into the parking

lot of a fast-food restaurant. After they picked up their fries and shakes, they went to a table away from the little kids and mothers who filled the front of the restaurant, so they could have a little privacy.

After they'd both settled into the booth and started to eat, Emily looked up. "I wanted to wait until we got here to tell you the real reason I wanted to see you. It's about Jed."

Caitlin looked up anxiously. "What about him?"

Emily spoke quietly. "We had a long talk over the weekend. He's really upset, Caitlin."

"Well? I'm really upset, too, Emily."

"He told me he'd seen you with Ian down at the stables, putting him on your horse—"

"He saw that?" Caitlin interrupted, amazed.

"He watched you from behind some trees," Emily explained. "What he said was confidential, but the way he talked, I just think I have to tell you." Emily sighed. "I know you two had some kind of huge fight at the prom—he won't tell me what it was about, and I won't ask you— but I know how much you care about him, and I know how stubborn my cousin can be."

Emily took a breath and continued. "For some reason Jed felt you were only taking care of Ian for selfish reasons. Then when he saw you and Ian working together, he decided you must really care about the kid. He told me Saturday that he was seeing you differently now. When I asked him what that meant, he just mumbled that it didn't matter anymore."

Emily was frowning. "I told him he should talk to you—that you still really cared about him. He said, 'But she's got Laurence now.' I tried to explain to him that, as much as you like Laurence, you don't feel the same way about Laurence that you feel about him." Emily looked up in anguish. "Was I right to do that, Caitlin? I've been worried about that all weekend. I shouldn't have butted in. It wasn't my business."

"No, no," Caitlin said with as much calm as she could gather under the circumstances. "It's okay. I'm glad you told him." She looked down at her lap. "I like Laurence a lot, but I can never care about him the way I cared for Jed." She rubbed one nervous hand over her brow. "I don't think I'll ever care about anybody like I did Jed." Her voice broke. "But he doesn't love me anymore, Emily—even if he said all that stuff. A couple of weeks ago he said some awful things to me, and he's totally ignored me since school began. Now I see him with other girls all the time."

"I think he flirts with other girls because he feels so bad," Emily explained. "He told me that he's tried to date since he broke up with you—

Tara Langden, for one—but he couldn't. He kept thinking of you." Emily looked up and added honestly, "But after telling me all this he also said that he wasn't ready to talk to you because too many terrible things had happened."

"He's right, Emily." Caitlin forced back the sob in her throat. "I can't talk about it, either."

"That's okay, I understand."

At the sympathetic tone in Emily's voice, Caitlin broke down again. "I wish he'd just let me explain."

"He's proud, Caitlin. He doesn't like to show his feelings."

Caitlin nodded, then covered her face with her hands. She felt like crying but didn't want to in front of Emily.

"You *really* love him, don't you?" Emily asked.

Caitlin looked up, her eyes teary. "Love him? God, Emily, I can't live without him. My whole life is a mess. Everything I do lately turns out all wrong. I can't sleep at night. I do like Laurence a lot, but I'm always thinking about Jed."

Emily touched Caitlin's forearm gently. "It's okay. I know how you feel. I'll work on Jed when I can. He's got to come down to earth, too, and stop walking away from people who care about him. He doesn't give anybody a chance."

Caitlin was thinking that Jed *had* given her a chance and she'd blown it.

141

She listened to the rest of Emily's words. "He gets only so close, then he runs away. But I think I can persuade him to talk to you about whatever problems you two had."

"You really think so, Emily?" Caitlin asked skeptically.

Emily shrugged. "I'll try. You two *have* to talk. You're both miserable."

"I know." Caitlin nodded. But could all the talk in the world ever make Jed love her again?

13

Jed was just ahead of Caitlin in the cafeteria line the next morning. As she reached for a container of orange juice, he turned his head and looked right at her. Remembering Emily's words, she smiled and nodded a hello. There was almost a question in his eyes as he studied her for an instant. Then he looked away, and without a word he picked up his tray and walked off.

Caitlin walked to her usual table, slamming her tray down with a thump. Emily must have been wrong, she concluded. Jed certainly wasn't acting as if he still had some feeling for her. But she didn't have time to dwell on it because just then Roger walked up to the table and sat in one of the empty chairs facing her.

"Time to talk picnic," he told her. "I've got to

straighten out a few details before this weekend."

Despite the personal problems on her mind, Caitlin nodded. "Okay, Roger, what do you need?"

"The site's okay, right?"

"No problem as I told you before. I'm not sure how we'll get there, though."

"I did arrange for some buses," Roger said. "But I'll need directions."

"I'll give them to you this afternoon," Caitlin said. "And what about food?"

"Everyone can bring their own." Roger shrugged.

"But everyone can't! Most of the kids can't go home and pack a picnic—they live too far away. Where are *they* going to get the food?"

"From the cafeteria?" Roger asked innocently.

"Are you serious?" Caitlin exclaimed. "We've got to have something good. How about having a huge order of fried chicken cooked up by the caterer in Martinsville?"

"Yeah, that sounds good."

"You'll need sodas and chips and plates and utensils, too."

"I'll have the guys pick them up."

"By the way, this is very late to be planning the picnic. What happened to Morgan? This should have been done a week ago. Hasn't she done anything?"

"I don't think so. I heard from Kim that some guy she met in Maine has been visiting. She hasn't been spending much time on campus," Roger growled.

Now she understood Roger's frustration. "Okay, Roger, I'll help you get it together. I'll call the caterer and get some fried chicken. You get the sodas, a half dozen cases, mixed."

"Yeah."

"And you're sure the buses are all set?"

"What do you take me for, Caitlin?"

"Roger," Caitlin said, looking up at him with her persuasive blue eyes, "I'm sorry. I've just got a lot on my mind."

"Don't we all," he said, sighing. "Okay. I'll talk to you in a couple of days."

The next day Caitlin plunged into the picnic arrangements. She called the catering place in Martinsville and arranged for enough chicken to feed the senior class, as well as cole slaw, rolls, and fruit. She knew there was plenty of money in the class treasury to cover the expense.

Caitlin didn't consult with Morgan on her plans, not even after Morgan's friend left. But

Caitlin was grateful when Laurence volunteered to help her with the arrangements.

"We should have some games," Caitlin told Laurence as they sat in the lounge studying together that night. "How about volleyball? It'll be too cool to swim—and I'm not even sure there's a pond there, anyway."

"I'll talk to one of the coaches. There's got to be a net we can borrow. I've got a bunch of Frisbees I could bring."

"Great! And try to get balls, bats, and mitts so we can play softball, too."

"Okay, chief." Laurence chuckled. "What's this place like?" he asked. "Hilly, a lot of trees?"

"Well, as I said, I haven't been there in years, but I remember it being pretty wooded with some open fields." She was thoughtful for a moment. "We'll need blankets!"

"Everyone should be able to bring their own," Laurence suggested. "They can take one off their beds, if nothing else."

The next day Caitlin told Roger about everything she'd arranged.

"You're kidding," he said in amazement. "You've done all that in two days?"

Caitlin shrugged as if it had been simple. "I've left one thing for you to do besides getting the soda. We'll need some chaperones, since this is a school-sponsored event."

"No problem. I'll take care of it. And thanks, Caitlin. Thanks a lot! You're a lifesaver.

The following Friday morning the seniors gathered in front of the main building ready to board the three waiting buses.

Caitlin had had the caterer in Martinsville deliver the food to the school. Then they loaded it onto one of the buses along with the rest of the things Roger had gotten.

Caitlin knew Jed was somewhere in the crowd, but she refused to look for him. Staying by Laurence's side, she climbed into the first bus without looking around to see who else was getting on.

Nevertheless, as the bus filled, she couldn't help but notice who was boarding. She was relieved Jed wasn't among them, and she relaxed a little as the buses started down the long Highgate drive and away from the school.

An hour later they approached the picnic spot. The foothills of the Blue Ridge Mountains loomed around them as the buses took the dirt roads off the highway.

Caitlin looked out the bus windows in confusion. The area around them looked nothing like what she'd remembered.

"This is so different," she said to Laurence. "There used to be pine forests here."

147

"Well, there's some trees out there," Laurence commented as he studied the new growth of pines pushing up here and there through the rocky ground. But that new greenery couldn't disguise the barren areas that mining had cut out of the once-beautiful land. There were slag heaps, upon which nothing grew, jutting up between the pines. Abandoned tunnels marred the hillsides, though in the years since the mines had been active, a growth of brush and grass had partially disguised some of the ugliness.

"I feel terrible, Laurence," she whispered. "I didn't remember it being like this. If I'd *known*—"

"The other side of the road looks okay," Laurence observed, trying hard to console her.

Quickly she glanced out the opposite windows of the bus and saw that part of the hillside hadn't been damaged so badly. The original, majestic pines still stood there with new growth springing up around, and there was an open, flat meadow with a stream running down its side. Caitlin breathed a sigh of relief.

The buses parked, and as Caitlin and Laurence disembarked, she quickly found Roger.

"Let's set up over there in that meadow," she said, pointing.

He nodded, but there was a scowl on his face. He motioned back over his shoulder to the hillside behind the buses. "Is this your idea of a joke, Caitlin?"

"I didn't know it looked this bad, Roger. Honestly."

"We would have been better off going to the state park," Roger declared.

"I'm sorry, Roger. I had no idea my grandmother's mining would ruin the land like this. Believe me, it used to be beautiful." She sighed. "Anyway, that field over there is still nice."

It took several minutes to get all the food and gear off the buses and set up the picnic at the far side of the meadow near the pines. From that vantage point, little could be seen of the ugliness of the mine ruins.

Laurence, Tim, and Matt set up the volleyball nets, while others, with the help of the three faculty members, spread out blankets and distributed the picnic baskets.

As Caitlin was carrying some of the soda over to the stream to keep it cold, Morgan came up to her. "Great place you picked," she said sarcastically.

"Don't rub it in, Morgan. If it hadn't been for me, we wouldn't be having a picnic at all."

"That's just like you, Caitlin. Taking over everything," Morgan continued in her nasty tone. "I thought I was supposed to be in charge of this picnic."

"You were, Morgan, but since you didn't do anything, Roger asked me to help."

"Roger asked you? Are you sure you didn't go sticking your nose in, telling him how it should be done?"

"I got involved only *after* I'd asked why you hadn't gotten it organized. Since you were too busy with your boyfriend from Maine, I said I'd help."

"You always have to be the boss, don't you?" Morgan sneered.

"Oh, get lost, Morgan. If you'd taken charge as you were supposed to, I wouldn't have had to do it *for* you!" With that she stomped away. She didn't care if Morgan wanted to run the rest of the picnic. She'd had enough.

Caitlin went to her blanket and opened up a picnic basket, which she shared with Laurence, Ginny, Bert, Jessica, Gloria, and Tim.

"This chicken's great!" Tim exclaimed as he grabbed his fourth drumstick. "Did you make it yourself, Caitlin?"

Despite her glum mood, she laughed. "Are you kidding? I would've had to have been cooking for the past three days."

"Does your grandmother own all this land?" Bert asked.

Caitlin was almost too embarrassed to answer, but finally nodded.

"Too bad mining has to make such a mess of things," Bert continued. "It must have been beautiful here once."

Caitlin saw Ginny give Bert a jab with her elbow. He reddened, realizing his mistake. "Sorry, Caitlin. I know it doesn't have anything to do with you."

"I don't like the way it looks here, either," she admitted. "It wasn't like this the last time I was here."

"Who's going to play volleyball with me after we eat?" Laurence asked quickly, knowing how uncomfortable the conversation was making Caitlin.

"We're playing." Gloria volunteered for herself and Tim. "Caitlin?"

Caitlin loved volleyball, but her disappointment over the ruined land and the possibility that Jed might play made her want to stay as far away from the crowd as she could. "Maybe later," she answered. "I thought I'd take a walk first. Do you mind, Laurence?"

"No, in fact, I'll come with you. I'd like to take a look around myself."

Soon they'd emptied the huge picnic basket, right down to the last pickle and potato chip. Everyone pitched in to clean up before wandering off to the various picnic activities.

After the others left, Laurence asked Caitlin, "Where do you want to go?"

"How about heading up the hill a little?"

"Sure."

They walked around the edge of the meadow and began climbing the hill. "Remember the last picnic we had?" Laurence asked quietly.

"Mmm, with Diana." Caitlin thought back to the day in August when Diana had recovered enough to make her first trip away from the hospital. Laurence and Caitlin had surprised her with a picnic at the state park. "That was fun."

"Today will be fun, too. Don't let the mine ruins bother you."

"But it looks so terrible. What are the other kids thinking?" She sighed, then added with determination, "I've made up my mind. I'm going to talk to my grandmother about it. She won't like hearing it, but it's wrong to tear up the land like this. There must be some way of putting it back the way it was." She pointed to their right. "Look at that slag heap. All of that rock was inside this hill once."

"But it's not your fault."

"I'm a Ryan. Ryan Mining's going to be my responsibility someday if my grandmother has her way. I just wonder how many other places have been left looking like this!"

As she was speaking, they passed the opening

152

to one of the abandoned tunnels. "I'm going to look inside," Caitlin said firmly.

"I don't think that's such a good idea," Laurence said cautiously.

"If I'm going to talk to my grandmother, I have to know all the facts—such as the condition of the inside of the tunnels," she told him.

"But it could be dangerous in there."

Caitlin didn't care. She stepped into the gaping hole, and Laurence reluctantly followed after her. There was enough light filtering in from the entrance of the tunnel to brighten the rock-walled interior and allow them to see the rotting support beams bracing the roof over their heads. The tunnel sloped down slightly as it progressed into the mountain, and Caitlin followed the narrow path to see what lay inside.

About ten yards in, there was a side tunnel, branching out to the left, that had begun to collapse. Rocks and debris had slid out, littering the floor of the main tunnel. Caitlin could hear a slight dripping sound from inside the blocked side tunnel. It sounded as if a small spring had eroded a passage through the crumbled rock.

She started to climb over some of the rocks.

Laurence followed behind her. "I don't know how much farther you can go. It looks like there's a cave-in just ahead."

"I want to try—"

Her words were cut short as Laurence suddenly tripped over one of the stones and lost his footing. He fell sideways, his shoulder crashing into one of the old support beams at the side of the tunnel. The beam cracked ominously and began to sag slowly.

"Laurence, watch out!" Caitlin screamed, jumping back and reaching for his arm.

But her warning came too late. The support beam gave way, as well as the debris behind it. A shower of pebbles and small rocks descended around him, one large rock striking him on the side of the head. The force of the blow knocked him over, and the rest of the loosened rock and gravel slid down onto the tunnel floor, almost burying Laurence.

"No!" Caitlin screamed. Already blood was flowing from the gash the rock had made on Laurence's forehead. His eyes were closed, and he wasn't moving.

Caitlin bent over him, grasped him under his arms, and tried to pull him free. But she couldn't budge him. She needed help quickly! She was afraid to leave him in case there was another slide, yet she knew she couldn't get him out by herself.

Praying Laurence would be all right until she got back, Caitlin rushed back out of the tunnel and into the sunshine on the hillside above the meadow. She could see her classmates playing volleyball and softball in the distance, but they were too far away to hear her cry. Then she spotted two boys throwing a Frisbee back and forth directly below her.

"Help!" she screamed. "Help! Laurence is trapped in the tunnel. Help me!"

They turned around, searching for the source of the call.

"Up here! Up on the hill!" She waved her arms frantically. They saw her. One of them was Jed, she realized with a combined thrill of dread and happiness.

"Hurry! There was a cave-in. I can't get him out!"

Immediately they scrambled up the incline. She barely waited for them to reach her before she turned back toward the tunnel. "In here. He's hurt!"

Her feet flew over the packed floor of the mine as the two boys pounded after her. She felt a wave of relief when she saw there'd been no further cave-in, but Laurence was still unconscious and bleeding badly.

"Geez," Jed cried. "Brett, help me dig him out and lift him!"

"I'll help, too," Caitlin said breathlessly.

"No, get outside!" Jed ordered. "The whole thing could come down."

But Caitlin wouldn't listen. She stayed in the tunnel with Jed and Brett as they maneuvered Laurence's limp body out from under the slide.

"Let's get out of here," Jed said urgently as he gently supported Laurence's legs, while Brett lifted his upper body. Laurence moaned as his eyes flickered open suddenly.

"Caitlin—" he mumbled.

"I'm fine, Laurence—"

Her words were cut short as the rock wall beside her shifted again. With a roaring rumble, part of the roof gave way and cascaded down into the few feet of space that separated Caitlin from the others. She stared disbelievingly as she saw the rocks pile up in front of her, raising a thick, dark cloud of dust that nearly choked her. But that wasn't the worst. Suddenly she heard a rush of water and felt the cold liquid swirling up around her ankles. There'd been more than a spring dripping behind the rocks blocking the side tunnel. There'd been a huge reservoir of trapped water. Freed from the side tunnel, it gushed out in a mad, swirling torrent all around her.

In sheer and utter terror, Caitlin screamed.

14

"Caitlin! *Caitlin!*" Jed yelled in anguish.

Caitlin could hear his panicked cry through the barrier of rocks between them.

"Jed!" she screamed, terrified by the darkness that now engulfed her. Near the top of the slide, she managed to see the faintest glimmer of light. She tried to scramble up the rocks, toward the light, but her feet kept slipping on the loose gravel. "I'm here, Jed. I'm here! Help me!"

"Caitlin. Thank God, you're alive!" he shouted. "Are you hurt?"

"No, but there's water in here. It's filling up the tunnel!"

"Oh, no!" she could hear him say to Brett. "Can you carry Laurence out yourself?"

Laurence moaned again. "Caitlin—"

"Don't worry, Laurence, I'll get her out," Jed said. "Even if it kills me."

She could hear Laurence groan, followed by Brett saying, "Come on, buddy, let's get you out of here."

"Get some more help!" Jed called anxiously. Then Caitlin heard stones being pulled away on the other side of the rockslide. "Climb up as high as you can, Caitlin," Jed ordered, taking firm control. "There's a small opening at the top. I'm going to try to widen it."

"Yes, Jed, yes. I'm climbing." But so was the water, she noted. It was rising around her calves, icy cold.

Terrified, she made her way little by little up the pile of rock toward the opening near the top. She could hear Jed frantically tearing away stones and rocks from the other side. Finally, her head was near the level of the small opening. For an instant she was free of the water, but it was swiftly following behind her, rising inch after inch, until it was again swirling around her feet.

Peering through the narrow opening, she saw a small portion of Jed's face. What she could see of his expression showed his worry and fear—and something else. Caring?

"Jed," she called through the opening.

He turned to her, his green eyes burning with intensity and determination. "Caitlin," he said n a whisper. "God, I was scared. Are you all ight?"

"So far."

"Start pulling some of the rocks away from your side. If we can get this opening a little wider, you can squeeze through."

"I'll try." Gripping the rocks with one hand, she began trying to widen the hole. The smaller rocks and gravel slid away easily, but there were bigger stones that she couldn't move. Her fingers were scratched raw as she clawed away at the barrier, but she felt no pain. Seeing Jed on the other side of the slide eased some of her terror.

He called to her. "Caitlin, there's one big stone in the way. If we can move it, the opening will be wide enough for you to get out. Can you feel it? It should be right in front of you."

"I feel it," she said hoarsely.

"Push at it. I'll pull from this side."

Caitlin pushed with all her strength. "It won't move."

"Try again—harder!"

The icy, black water was up to her thighs, and she couldn't climb any higher.

"It's no use, Jed," she cried. "The water keeps coming."

"I know. It's seeping through this side, too. Push!" he ordered. "I've got a better grip on it."

With tears streaming down her cheeks, she

tried again. She thought the rock had moved a tiny fraction, but she was too panic-stricken to know whether or not that was just wishful thinking. The water had risen to her waist. "Go, Jed! Save yourself. It's hopeless!"

"I'm not leaving you!" he growled.

"The whole wall could come down on you!"

"Let me worry about that."

"Why are you doing this? You hate me. Why are you risking your life to save me?"

He didn't answer. "Push again! It's starting to move!"

She was shaking from the cold of the water, which had risen to her waist.

"Jed," she cried urgently, "I just want you to know—if anything happens to me—if I die, I'm so sorry. I've tried so hard to undo all the bad things I've done. Please believe me, Jed. I've already told Ian and the Fosters, so they wouldn't hate Diana anymore."

"You're not going to die, Caitlin! I won't let you. Push one more time!"

The rock slid slightly toward Jed. She heard him scramble for a better position. He pulled again. The stone moved under Caitlin's fingertips, and she pushed again with all her strength.

"Okay! Okay," Jed called. "I can work it free now from this side."

But would there be time? The water was continuing to rise.

Suddenly the rock rolled free, down the slope f the slide away from her. Caitlin saw Jed's face nd upper torso as he crouched on the slide. here was an expression of incredible relief on is face.

He reached through the opening toward her. Easy," he whispered as she grabbed his hands nd slithered her upper body through the narow opening. He grabbed her by the waist, and ith his strong arms, helped her the rest of the ay through. She felt some jagged edges of tone scrape her legs, but she clenched her teeth nd refused to cry out.

Finally her knees touched the stone outside he opening, and she was able to scramble the est of the way out. Jed's arm gripped her tightly s they slid down the rocks to the tunnel floor. or a brief instant as they stood on the firm round, they looked into each other's eyes, and hen they fell into each other's arms.

But their joy was only momentary. The water ad surged to the height of the opening they'd nade, and the pressure of it forced an even vider opening through the gravel. The icy water ascaded down toward them like an exploding vaterfall.

"Run!" Jed cried, grabbing her arm and pulling her after him.

The force of the water hitting the back of their highs nearly knocked them over, but Jed held

Caitlin's arm firmly. They ran up the slight grade of the tunnel not stopping until they were out in the sunlight and had dragged themselves to slightly higher ground. They were dripping wet and shaking, but safe.

The wave of water had followed swiftly behind them, and a stream escaped from the mouth of the tunnel and continued down the hillside.

Caitlin and Jed fell down together on the rocky hillside, staring at the mouth of the tunnel, too exhausted and shocked from their experience to speak. They clung together as if they were afraid to let go. Jed hugged Caitlin against him, and she sighed deeply, feeling the warmth of his body through her wet clothing.

She felt safe in Jed's arms—the arms she'd been longing to have hold her for so long. He'd saved her life, risking his own to do it. She didn't know why. There was so much they had to say to each other, but for the moment she just wanted to savor the feeling of being held by him.

"Oh, Caitlin." His fingers tangled in her hair. "I almost lost you."

"You saved my life," she said in a shocked whisper. She closed her arms tighter around his broad, strong back. "I—I was so scared!"

"It's okay now. Everything's going to be all right."

"Oh, Jed," she began, "I—"

Her words were interrupted by the sound of voices as two state troopers ran up the hillside toward them. Apparently someone had radioed for help from one of the buses.

"There they are!" the state trooper in the lead called as he approached them. He glanced toward the tunnel at the water that continued rushing out and shook his head. "Looks like you had an awful time in there!"

Caitlin and Jed nodded. Then Caitlin suddenly remembered Laurence and sat up straight. "Laurence! Is he all right?" Instantly she felt Jed stiffen beside her.

"You mean the other boy?" He didn't wait for a response. "They're taking him to the hospital. How are you two?"

"I'm fine," Jed said quickly and firmly. "But I don't know about her. She was trapped."

Two emergency paramedics came up the hill just then and knelt down beside Caitlin and Jed. "Any head injuries?" one of the paramedics asked.

"No," Caitlin answered. *Just go away*, she added silently. *Leave Jed and me alone. We have to talk.*

Jed quickly shook his head in response to their question.

"Any pain?"

Again they shook their heads.

"She was in the water for a while," Jed volunteered.

"But I'm okay." Caitlin was bleeding a little from cuts and abrasions on her hands. Her jeans legs were ripped from when she'd slid through the opening in the rocks, and there was a long scratch on one leg.

"Let's get you to the hospital and check you out, just to be sure."

With a paramedic assisting each of them, they rose and started down the hillside.

The state trooper walked beside them with his book open. "Can you describe what happened? I'll need the information for my report."

Caitlin didn't even want to think about it, but she realized the trooper was only doing his job. "Laurence and I went into the tunnel," Caitlin began. "He tripped and fell against one of the supports." She shuddered at the memory. "The beam cracked. The next thing I knew, the rocks were flying at us. I saw what was happening first and jumped back. I tried to pull Laurence out of the way, but he was the closest. One of the rocks hit him in the head—" She couldn't go on. Her eyes had filled with tears. She tried to wipe them from her cheeks.

When Jed saw her tears, he looked away quickly.

By the time the trooper had questioned both of them on the details of the accident, they'd reached the bottom of the hill, where an ambulance was waiting for them. The rest of the senior class and the faculty chaperones were gathered at the edge of the field, watching nervously. Caitlin gazed blindly at the sea of curious and worried faces.

"You kids were lucky," the trooper said when he'd finished his report. "But you ought to have known better than to go into an abandoned mine." He chuckled. "Making out, huh?"

"No!" Caitlin shouted. "The mine belongs to my grandmother."

The trooper raised his eyebrows. "So you're a Ryan? I'd better get in touch with your grandmother right away."

Caitlin was silent as she stepped up into the ambulance. What had happened to the closeness she and Jed had shared just a few minutes before? She'd been sure Jed would at least want to ride with her and keep her company. They had so much to talk about. But she felt too self-conscious under the watchful eyes of the paramedics to call out to him.

A moment later someone shut the rear door, separating her from Jed, and she was whisked away to the hospital.

15

Gordon Westlake had been waiting in Regina Ryan's oak-paneled reception room since one o'clock that afternoon. He had tried numerous times to talk to her ever since the day he'd encountered Caitlin in the store. It had hurt him deeply to see further evidence of how his daughter had been turned against him. He was determined to insist that Regina Ryan stop lying to Caitlin and tell her granddaughter the truth about what had happened seventeen years earlier. But Regina Ryan had refused to take his calls. This time, however, he wasn't going to take no for an answer.

Quickly he glanced down at his watch. Two-twenty-five. Straightening the cuff on his jacket, he rose and approached the receptionist. "Is Mrs. Ryan ready to see me yet?" he asked.

True Love

The black-haired woman looked over her half glasses at Gordon Westlake. "I'll buzz again." She picked up the telephone and waited for Mrs. Ryan's answer. A moment later she relayed Dr. Westlake's message, nodded her head, then put down the receiver. "I'm sorry. Mrs. Ryan says she can't be disturbed right now."

"That's just too bad," Gordon Westlake said, his temper flaring. Stepping beyond the receptionist's desk, he reached for the brass door handle that led to Regina Ryan's inner office.

"What are you doing here?" Mrs. Ryan exclaimed, looking up from her desk as Gordon Westlake burst into the room.

"You haven't answered my phone calls, so I've come to talk with you in person," the handsome, dark-haired doctor said firmly.

"I fail to see what we have to discuss. We settled everything during the summer."

"Not to *my* satisfaction." Dr. Westlake stepped forward, leaned on the edge of Mrs. Ryan's desk, and faced her, his eyes flashing. "My daughter hates me because of the lies you have told her about me. You could never accept that Laura and I were in love, so you lied to her and turned her against me. But that wasn't enough for you! When Laura died giving birth to our daughter, you couldn't rest until Caitlin hated

167

me, too. You made her believe that I deserted her."

"You ruined Laura's life," Regina Ryan said, her mouth tight with hatred.

"Do you really believe that? Laura and I were very much in love. We were happy! We would have been married if you hadn't stepped in and dragged her off to Europe. Now you're doing the same thing to your granddaughter. You care nothing about the things that would make her happy. Your only concern is that she does what makes *you* happy!"

"Get out, Dr. Westlake!" Regina Ryan ordered.

"Not until you've heard everything I have to say. I want you to tell Caitlin the truth! I want her to be able to make a fair decision about whether to accept or reject me. She needs a loving parent. It doesn't take a great deal of insight to see how unhappy she is."

"You're crazy. Caitlin is perfectly happy!"

"And a convincing actress, I have a feeling. At least when she's around you. She is my *daughter*. I have a right to get to know her and give her love and support."

"You're being unrealistic!" Regina said stonily. "She's lived nearly seventeen years without a father or mother. To burden her with all of this now would be cruel!"

"The greater cruelty would be not telling her the truth."

"Leave well enough alone, Dr. Westlake. Caitlin is quite content. She is doing well at school, has found a very suitable boyfriend, is planning to study business in college—"

"So that she can take over Ryan Mining?" Dr. Westlake growled.

"I would hate to have to take legal action against you, Dr. Westlake," Regina threatened.

"Don't try to intimidate me—"

The buzzer on the desk phone interrupted them. "Sorry to interrupt you, Mrs. Ryan," the secretary called. "But there's an urgent phone call for you on line one."

Immediately she picked up the receiver. "Regina Ryan speaking."

As the conversation at the other end of the line proceeded, Regina Ryan's face gradually paled.

"An accident!"

There was a further silence as she listened. "The hospital in Winchester? Yes, I know it. Is she all right? Yes, I'll be there as soon as possible. Of course you have my permission to treat her!"

"What is it?" Dr. Westlake cried, sensing the conversation had to do with Caitlin.

"There's been an accident in one of the old

mine shafts," she said, rising from her chair. "Caitlin was trapped. She's been hurt."

"Mine shaft—I don't understand? What was she doing in a mine shaft?"

Mrs. Ryan spoke as though in a daze. "The senior class had an outing. Caitlin asked if they could use some of the mine company land in the West Virginia foothills. They're bringing her to the Winchester Hospital," she added, rushing to the office door. "I've got to go!"

"I'm coming with you!" Dr. Westlake stated firmly.

Too upset to protest, she allowed the doctor to follow her to the parking lot.

"We can go in my car," he said quickly, taking the older woman's arm. "You can't drive in the condition you're in." He helped her into the passenger seat, then ran around to the driver's side.

They lapsed into silence, each consumed with worry. Regina Ryan toyed with the rings on her fingers and stared out the windshield as the doctor swung the car onto the highway toward the hospital. She never should have given her permission for the senior class to use the land, she scolded herself. She hadn't been to the spot in years, but she should have known from experience what the site would be like—slag heaps and old tunnels that, more likely than not, were not boarded up.

Now she was paying the ultimate price. Her own granddaughter was hurt! The police had been so vague when they called. All they'd said was that Caitlin had been trapped. The thought of Caitlin buried beneath a pile of rock made Regina's hands shake. Not until that moment did she realize how dearly she loved her granddaughter or how much she'd taken her for granted. For the very first time, she realized that her life would have no meaning if anything happened to Caitlin.

But did Caitlin know that? The sudden thought that she might not made Mrs. Ryan shudder. As they rushed to the hospital, she kept thinking about the way she'd treated Caitlin and the cold, accusing words Dr. Westlake had thrown at her. He was right, she told herself, finally able to admit it. She understood now that the pain of her own daughter's death had caused her to hold Caitlin at arm's length and deny her any true affection. But it was insane—she *loved* Caitlin. Until that moment when her granddaughter's life was in danger, she hadn't allowed herself to admit just how much. Dr. Westlake was right—she had been selfish and uncaring of anyone's desires but her own.

Oh, if she only had it to do over, she cried to herself! If only she could go back and undo the wrongs and make up for her mistakes. God willing, she would have the chance!

16

The ambulance pulled up to the emergency room doors. An orderly opened the door, placed Caitlin in a wheelchair, and took her to an examining room. Caitlin didn't have long to wait before one of the staff doctors came in, glasses riding halfway down his nose. He looked at her and smiled. "Considering what you've just been through, you look pretty chipper, young lady," he said. "Any pain?"

"No."

"Dizziness?"

"No."

"Well, let's have a look at you, anyway." He patted the examination table beside the wheelchair, then helped her up from the chair onto the table. Quickly he examined her hands and the cuts on her legs, pressing gently over the bones.

"What were you doing in the mine shaft?" he asked.

"Exploring."

"Humph. Those mine people ought to be shot. You're lucky, young lady. I'd suggest you stay away from holes in the ground in the future."

Caitlin nodded as the doctor stuck a thermometer in her mouth, examined her eyes, listened to her heartbeat, and took her blood pressure.

"Looks good," he said finally, scribbling on the clipboard in his hand. "I'm going to have a nurse bandage up that cut on your leg. Just sit tight for a minute. Are you warm enough?"

Caitlin nodded. The jeans and cotton shirt that had gotten soaked in the mine were now nearly dry. She didn't feel uncomfortable.

"Okay, the nurse will be in soon."

"The other boy who was hurt, Laurence Baxter," she asked urgently. "Do you know how he is?"

Sensing her anxiety, the doctor smiled and patted her arm reassuringly. "Don't worry. He's going to be all right. We'll be keeping him here for observation, but I think after a day's rest in the hospital, we can ship him back to school again."

"Can I see him before I leave?"

"I think we could arrange it—only for a minute, though. Stop by the nurse's station when you're done here, and please don't leave the hospital until your parents or someone from the school comes for you." With that he was gone, and a few minutes later the nurse came in to clean and bandage Caitlin's leg.

Caitlin was just rising from the examination table when the door burst open. In shock Caitlin lay back down on the table as two people entered the room—her grandmother and her father.

Regina Ryan ran toward Caitlin and threw her arms around her granddaughter. Even in her amazed state, Caitlin saw the deep concern— almost anguish—on her grandmother's face. She'd never seen Regina look that worried, certainly never when it concerned her.

"Oh, Caitlin, I'm so glad you're alive. All the way here I was imagining the worst. Oh, look at your hands!"

"They'll be fine, Grandmother," Caitlin said distractedly as she stared over her grand-mother's shoulder to Dr. Westlake. "What's *he* doing here?" she asked icily.

"I was with your grandmother in her office when the call came about the accident," Dr. Westlake answered quietly, his eyes never leaving his daughter's face.

"What was he doing in your office?" Caitlin asked, facing her grandmother. "Why were you even talking to him?"

"I went to see your grandmother, Caitlin," her father continued firmly, "to talk to her—"

Caitlin didn't let him finish. She glared at him. "Can't you take no for an answer? I told you I never wanted to see you again. Why don't you leave me alone?"

For a moment Dr. Westlake hesitated. His face was white and pained, yet his eyes held a silent plea.

"You deserted me," Caitlin stormed. "You didn't care then! And now *I* don't care, either! Go away! Get out of my life!"

Dr. Westlake's hands were clenched in fists at his sides, but he only said in his deep, quiet voice, "I'm truly sorry that you feel that way, Caitlin. I've told you the truth about what happened, but if you can't believe me, then I'll leave you alone." He started to turn toward the door.

"Gordon, *wait*!" Regina Ryan called.

Filled with confusion, Caitlin stared at her grandmother. What was going on? Why had her grandmother suddenly taken such an interest in Dr. Westlake?

"I have something to say to both of you— something that should have been said a long

176

time ago." The older woman's hands were shaking; her lips trembled, but she gently took her granddaughter's hand. "Caitlin, I've been a bitter, selfish old woman. Hearing today that you'd been hurt, perhaps very seriously, made me realize how wrong I've been." Regina Ryan visibly seemed to sag. "What I told you about your father wasn't the truth. He didn't desert you. He didn't even know you existed until this summer."

Caitlin continued to stare at her grandmother in shock.

"When your mother and Gordon were in college, they were seriously involved with each other and wanted to marry. I didn't approve of their relationship. It would have meant your mother's possibly leaving Virginia and slaving to help a medical student through his internship. I had other plans for her. I told her some things that I'm ashamed to admit to now—unpleasant things about Gordon Westlake, which I made up to keep her from leaving.

"She believed every word I told her. Because of it, she broke off their engagement, and I took her to Europe. We'd been there for two months when Laura admitted to me that she was pregnant. Naturally I was infuriated, but I refused to let her notify Gordon. I planned to put the baby up for adoption after it was born.

"We moved to a quiet, out-of-the-way village and were doing quite nicely. But then came Laura's horrible delivery. As if suspecting she wasn't going to survive the birth, she made me promise to raise you.

"When she died, I was so devastated I could barely function. Laura was all I'd had, you see. I remained in Europe for several months, then brought you home and manufactured a story. I told people that Laura had married in Europe, but that after she'd died giving birth, her young husband had run off, leaving you with me. Seeing my grief, my friends readily accepted my story.

"But my anger and pain at the injustice of my daughter's death didn't go away so easily. I hated the man whose love had taken my daughter from me. I was determined to make sure he would never know the child who'd been born out of that love. It was my revenge."

The older woman's face was creased with guilt and remorse as she looked at Caitlin. "I was afraid that one day your paths might cross. I told you your father was a worthless, selfish man who'd left you in my care rather than accept the responsibility of raising you. It was a lie, Caitlin. Dr. Westlake didn't desert you." Regina's voice quavered. "I love you very much, Caitlin. I know I've never told you that, but I do. I can't ask you to forgive me after all I've done to hurt you, but please do not hate your father."

Caitlin was so stunned by her grandmother's confession, she couldn't speak. She looked from her grandmother to her father, who was watching her hopefully. She was remembering the night she'd seen her father in the shopping center. She'd been so cruel to him, yet here he was practically begging to be part of her life. Could it really be possible that he loved her? Was that what love meant—that he still cared about her despite her behavior toward him?

Of course it was, she realized. Wasn't that the way she felt about Jed—that burning desire to be with him even when he acted as if she didn't exist?

Her grandmother turned to Dr. Westlake. "Gordon, I want to apologize to you, too. I know these few words can't possibly come close to making up for all the damage I've done, but I'm sincerely sorry."

There was dead silence in the room as Regina Ryan finished speaking. Caitlin knew instinctively that her grandmother had finally told her the truth. Instead of reacting with anger to her grandmother's deception, she felt an almost overwhelming relief. She knew what it was to live with lies and guilt—always afraid, always putting off the admission of that guilt. But more important than that, she was overcome with the knowledge that she was loved! Caitlin realized her grandmother loved her enough to risk losing her to a father who had never rejected her.

She threw her arms around her grandmother's neck and hugged her tightly. "It's all right, Grandmother. It's all right."

Regina Ryan hugged her granddaughter in return. "Oh, my dear Caitlin, I've been so wrong. I love you so much!"

Gordon Westlake stepped closer, his eyes filled with tears of relief, gratitude, and appreciation. "Thank you, Regina," he said quietly. "I know the courage it took for you to say that."

Caitlin turned her head to look at her father. It was still a little difficult for her to accept that he truly cared about her. But she was willing to try; she could let herself get to know him. She smiled hesitantly. "I'm glad you're here, Father."

Her words made him beam. "I know it will take time, Caitlin, but I hope we can get to know each other and be a family."

Caitlin nodded, holding back tears of joy. "I'd like that, too."

Unsettled as Caitlin was, she still wanted to see Laurence before she left the hospital. While her father and grandmother waited in the lobby,

Caitlin talked to the nurse and found out where his room was.

Laurence was lying in bed with his forehead bandaged, but he was awake, and he smiled at her as she came in. Caitlin hurried to the bed.

"Hi." She smiled and took his hands. "How's your head?"

"A little sore, but not bad. How are *you*?"

"Okay. A couple of cuts and bruises, that's all."

"They didn't tell me much about what happened," Laurence said. "I came to in the tunnel when Jed and Brett were pulling me out, and then I heard a second cave-in. They said you were okay, but they couldn't give me any details."

"I'm okay, Laurence. I'm sorry I ever dragged you into the tunnel." Caitlin sighed miserably. "If I'd listened to you, none of this would have happened."

"But maybe it was meant to be," Laurence said softly.

"What do you mean?"

"I've been doing a lot of thinking—not just today, but for the last few weeks. I've been thinking about us and the way you react whenever you see Jed."

Caitlin opened her mouth to protest, but Laurence silenced her. "Wait. Let me finish. I care about you a lot, Caitlin, but I've known all along you didn't care for me the same way you care for Jed. It's okay. You never promised anything. But I've seen you when Jed's around—and today I was conscious long enough in the tunnel to see how *he* looked after the second slide, when he knew your life was in danger. He still loves you, Caitlin."

Caitlin again started to interrupt, but Laurence shook his head.

"I know you'd never hurt me by telling me you still love Jed. Because of that, I have a feeling you'd never break up with me, either." He took a breath and let it out slowly. "Now that I know that Jed loves you, too, I can't stand in your way. In time you'd start to resent me, and I couldn't take that."

"Laurence, Jed and I—" Caitlin stopped. She'd started to say, "Jed and I are finished," but everything had changed that day. Finally she said, "Laurence, I *do* care about you."

"I know you do, and I'll always be your friend—if you want me to."

"You know I do!"

"Go talk to Jed and straighten it out."

Caitlin started to cry, and Laurence reached out to hug her. "You're supposed to be smiling, not crying," he said softly.

"But I feel so awful. You deserve better than this."

"Don't worry. I'm going to be fine," he said.

"Why are you so good to me?"

He didn't answer.

A nurse stuck her head in the door. "Miss, you'll have to leave now. He needs his rest."

Hastily Caitlin wiped the tears from her cheeks. "Yes, I'm going."

"I'll see you back at school."

"Laurence, I don't know what to say."

"Don't say anything—just go find Jed."

17

By the time Caitlin reached the lobby, she had composed herself enough so that her grandmother and father wouldn't see her tears.

Regina Ryan looked as if she'd aged five years in the last hour, yet there was also a new lightness in her manner.

"How's Laurence?" she asked worriedly when Caitlin reached them.

"Fine," she said, deciding to hold off the news of their breakup until later. "He has some stitches in his forehead, but the doctor says he'll be okay. Probably he'll leave the hopsital tomorrow."

Regina Ryan sighed heavily but made no further comment.

"Ready to head back to Highgate?" her father asked.

Caitlin looked up at him and nodded. He seemed so tall and strong as he stood next to her, someone she could depend on if she needed to. But she still felt awkward with him.

The three made their way out of the lobby of the modern hospital and down the short walk to the parking lot. "We're right over here," Gordon Westlake said, indicating with his hand.

They'd barely started across the parking lot when they were met by Dean Foster, who was pushing Ian in his wheelchair.

"Caitlin!" Ian called.

Caitlin could hardly believe it. "What are you doing here?" she cried. Her attention focused on the little boy. He'd called to her. Did that mean he'd forgiven her?

Dean Foster stopped beside them and said a little breathlessly, "You're all right—thank heavens! And how are Laurence and Jed?"

"They're okay. Laurence is still in the hospital."

"I rushed to get here. I was out running an errand when the call came from the police. Elaine took the message, and I came over as soon as I could." He glanced at his small son as he spoke softly to the adults. "Elaine didn't realize Ian had heard us, and he was nearly hysterical when he heard you'd been hurt. This isn't the place for him, I know, but now that he's

185

seen that you're fine—" He leaned down to his son, speaking louder, "You see, Ian, Caitlin isn't hurt—"

But as he spoke, a miracle was happening.

While everyone was listening to Dean Foster, Ian had risen from his wheelchair.

In his excitement to see Caitlin, he walked the four short steps between Caitlin and his wheelchair and threw his arms around her hips. "Caitlin, I missed you!" the little boy cried. "I missed you so much! I was scared you were hurt!"

For a moment everyone stared at Ian in amazement.

"Ian, you walked!" Caitlin was the first to cry out, kneeling quickly and hugging the little boy close to her chest. "You *walked*! You see, I knew you could do it!" Dean Foster knelt by his son as well and wrapped his arms around him.

"I'm so happy, Ian!" Caitlin tried to hold back her tears of joy.

Dean Foster was beyond speech. He just kept smiling as he held his son. "That's the way, son," he finally said in a choked voice.

"Daddy, you don't have to cry." Ian frowned in confusion. "Don't be so sad."

Dean Foster gave his son a wobbly smile. "I'm not sad, Ian. Sometimes people cry when they're happy, too, and I'm very happy!"

186

Ian grinned, then suddenly his eyes widened as if he'd just at that moment realized himself what he'd accomplished. "I walked, Daddy," he said with excitement.

"You sure did."

"It didn't hurt as much as I thought it would."

"And it will hurt less and less the more you practice," his father reassured him.

Ian was grinning proudly. Then unexpectedly his small brow furrowed in distress, and he glanced pleadingly at Caitlin. "Will you come back and baby-sit for me? Please? You can be my friend again. I'm sorry I said you weren't."

"Oh, Ian." Caitlin sighed. "Of course, I'll come back. I've missed you so much."

"Can I ride Duster again?"

"Maybe all by yourself now."

Caitlin felt as if her heart were about to burst with happiness. Ian had forgiven her, and better than that, he finally was recovering. All the hours she'd spent with him had been worthwhile.

"My legs are getting tired," Ian said.

His father immediately started to pick him up, but Caitlin made a move to stop him. "Do you think, Ian," she asked encouragingly, "that if I held one hand and your father the other, you could walk back to your chair?"

"Okay." With his hands held firmly, the boy

took the four slow, awkward steps back to the wheelchair.

"It won't be long before you're out running and playing ball with the other kids, Ian," his father said with delight.

"Can we play baseball?"

"We sure can!"

Dean Foster settled Ian back into the wheelchair and tousled his blond curls. He then drew Caitlin aside and whispered to her.

"Thank you." The words were so deeply sincere and grateful that Caitlin felt humbled. "Elaine told me what happened," he added quietly. "I was angry at first, but I can see you've done everything in your power to make amends. Elaine and I both want you to know that you're welcome to come back and work with Ian."

Regina Ryan smiled at Dean Foster. "I'm so happy for you, Richard."

"It's not often we get to witness miracles," Gordon Westlake added.

Caitlin interrupted suddenly. "Dean Foster, you haven't met my father, Dr. Gordon Westlake. Father, Dean Foster."

For an instant the Dean's surprise showed on his face, but Caitlin quickly flashed him a look that told him she'd explain everything later. Dean Foster then took Gordon Westlake's extended hand. "How do you do. It's a pleasure to meet you!"

"Nice to meet you, too."

"You're a medical doctor?" Richard Foster asked.

"Yes, which is why I can appreciate you son's accomplishment. Too often I see endings that aren't quite so happy."

"And if it weren't for Caitlin's help, I don't know if he would have taken those steps so soon. This could have been a day of tragedy," Richard Foster mused. "Instead it's turned out to be a day of miracles."

Caitlin grinned. "I'll see you back at Highgate, Ian." She bent over and kissed his cheek.

"Will you come over today?"

"Tomorrow. It'll be too late when we get back."

"You promise?"

"I promise!"

Caitlin was still glowing from Ian's success when she and her grandmother got into Dr. Westlake's car for the drive back to Ryan Mining and then to Highgate.

"This has been quite a day," Regina Ryan mused, echoing her granddaughter's thoughts.

"That it has," Gordon Westlake agreed, smiling broadly. "But, except for the mine accident, I wouldn't change any of it!"

"I'm so happy for the Fosters. Their son's injury has been a great burden on them." Mrs. Ryan smiled at her granddaughter. "And I'm very proud of you, dear."

They reached the turn-off for the Ryan Mining offices, and Gordon Westlake pulled into the parking lot to drop Regina Ryan at her car. Before she climbed out, she leaned over and hugged Caitlin around the shoulders.

"Your father and I were talking at the hospital," she said. "We'd like for the three of us to have dinner together this weekend and get to know one another better. Would you like that?"

"You know I would." Caitlin returned her grandmother's kiss.

"We'll talk before then and arrange the time." She looked over at the man who would have been her son-in-law. "Gordon, again I am sorry for all the trouble I've caused. I'll try to make up for it." She opened the door and stepped from the car. "Drive safely."

She closed the door and walked away, the dignity back in her posture and stride.

As Caitlin and her father continued to High-gate, he asked her about the school, her interests, her friends. The self-consciousness between them began to vanish.

"You do a lot of riding, I gather," he commented.

"Yes. I love it. Do you ride?"

"Not by your standards." He chuckled. "I've taken a few jogs on horseback now and then, and come away limping the next day. I play a decent game of tennis, though."

"Great, we can play sometime. And, if you want, I'll teach you to ride." Caitlin had to smile to herself at the suggestion of giving her father riding lessons.

But the idea didn't seem to bother him in the least. "That would be fun." He paused thoughtfully. "This isn't really the time to bring it up, but maybe you'd like to think about coming to spend a weekend or two with me."

Caitlin saw the love and tenderness in his expression and was warmed. "I'd like that, too."

"Good." He grinned.

The prospect of getting to know her father was so wonderful, Caitlin was almost afraid to believe it would actually happen. Dr. Westlake was genuinely interested in her. And he was an interesting man in his own right. Caitlin was beginning to realize the pain *he'd* been suffering since her rejection of him. But they'd make up for that in the time they had ahead, and it was a time she now looked forward to.

Before he dropped her at her dorm, he made

one last comment. "Caitlin, I hope you realize how much courage it took for your grandmother to say what she did today. I hope you can forgive her for all the past wrongs. She's suffered, too."

"I've already forgiven her." Then, a little shyly, Caitlin leaned over and gave her father a kiss on the cheek.

18

Caitlin was desperate as she ran up to her room. For the past hour she'd been looking all over for Jed. She'd been to his dorm, and questioned his friends, but no one knew where he was.

Caitlin burst into her room, and Ginny came running over to her. She put her arms around her friend. "God, are you okay? I've been waiting for you to get back. There've been all kinds of rumors flying around, but no one seemed to know exactly what had happened. People have been coming by for the last hour, asking when you were coming back."

"I'm okay, Ginny," Caitlin answered breathlessly. "Have you seen Jed? I've been looking all over for him and can't find him."

"No, I haven't seen him, Caitlin. But why are you so anxious to see him?"

"I need to talk to him, Ginny. He saved my life!"

"What happened?"

"I haven't got time!"

"Yes, you do. You've got to calm down."

Caitlin gave a deep sigh and tried to relax. Ginny was right. She was so upset she was shaking.

"Do you know about Laurence?" she asked in a rushed voice.

"Brett told us. Is Laurence going to be okay?"

"Yes. He'll be back here tomorrow probably."

"Brett also said there was another cave-in, and you were trapped, but then we saw you walk to the ambulance and get in."

Quickly Caitlin described the second cave-in scene to Ginny. "I thought it was hopeless, but Jed wouldn't leave. Finally, we broke through, and he dragged me away. Once we were out of the tunnel, Jed hugged me, Ginny. It was as if he didn't want to let me go, as if he still loved me! It felt so wonderful to know he cared. I wanted to talk to him, but the police and paramedics came, and there wasn't any chance."

"Okay. We've got to find him. Have you tried his dorm?"

Caitlin nodded. "Matt told me one of the state troopers brought him back there, but he hadn't seen him for hours."

"He's probably as shaky as you are. Where do you think he'd go if he wanted to just be alone?"

Suddenly Caitlin had a thought. "Do you think he'd go to the soccer field? It'd be deserted at this time of day."

"It's worth a try."

Caitlin didn't even take the time to wash her face or straighten her hair. She ran out of the dorm.

Since it was close to dinner time, the campus was empty as Caitlin ran across the lawn toward the soccer field. She hadn't even thought of what she was going to say to Jed. There was so much to say. She was so afraid he'd had second thoughts about the way he'd treated her after they'd escaped from the tunnel. She felt as if she'd die if he rejected her again.

She reached the edge of the downgrade behind the campus buildings and looked down toward the soccer field. One lone figure sat on a bench to the side of the field. Caitlin didn't have to get any closer to know it was Jed.

Slowing her pace, she started down the hill. The thick grass muffled her footsteps. Jed didn't hear her until she was standing directly beside him. She laid a hand gently on his shoulder.

He lifted his head from his hands and gazed up at her. A ray of sunlight danced on her glistening black hair. Her eyes were soft and filled with both love and longing.

A spark of hope suddenly lit his own green eyes when he saw her.

"I've been looking all over for you," she whispered. "I had to talk to you, Jed. I wanted to talk to you in the ambulance, but you didn't ride with me. Why?"

"I wanted to talk to you, too," he said.

"So much happened in the hospital. My grandmother came with my father, and she told us how she'd lied all these years. My father never deserted me—he never even knew I had been born! And then when we were leaving, Ian and Dean Foster came across the parking lot. Ian was afraid that I'd been hurt, and when he saw me, he walked to me. Only four steps, but he's going to be okay!"

"Thank God for that," Jed said. "You must be happy." His voice sounded lifeless.

"Oh, I am, Jed, I am!"

"I looked for you in the hospital."

Caitlin was struck speechless for a moment. "You did?" she asked finally.

"I had one of the troopers drive me there just so I could check on how you were."

"So why didn't you come see me?"

"When I asked where you were, they told me you were with Laurence." Jed turned away.

Caitlin thought he looked defeated. "I can't compete with him."

"He broke up with me," Caitlin announced.

Startled, Jed stared at her.

"He said he knew I still loved you," she continued.

Jed swallowed. "Do you?"

"Yes. As much as I care about him, I could never have loved him the way I love you." Her voice trembled. "But it didn't seem to matter what I felt for you because you've hated me since last June."

"I don't hate you anymore, Caitlin."

It was Caitlin's turn to stare. "You don't?"

He looked into her eyes. "No. I've seen that you're sorry for what you did and that you've been trying to make up for it." He hesitated. "Diana pleaded with me to forgive you. And both she and Emily told me how much you were suffering. At first I didn't listen—I didn't want to. I kept avoiding you because I didn't want to believe you'd changed. I was afraid to trust you again.

"But during the past few weeks it's become harder and harder for me. After I saw you that day with Ian, I realized I had misjudged you. You *had* changed. I also realized I still loved you, anyway. I couldn't stop—"

"Jed—" Caitlin began.

Suddenly Jed was on his feet and wrapping his arms around her. "Oh, Caitlin." He sighed. "When you were trapped in the tunnel, I realized how much I need you, and that if anything should happen to you—"

"I was thinking the same thing. You saved my life, but if you'd gotten hurt or—"

"I was saving my own life, too. Caitlin, I can't live without you." He ran his fingers through her hair, touched his lips to her forehead.

"I love you so much, Jed. I've been so miserable since you left."

"I think we've both been miserable. I tried to tell myself I never wanted to have anything to do with you again. I tried dating other girls, but it didn't work. I kept wishing I were with you instead."

"That's how I felt with Laurence, though I'll always be grateful for his friendship. He was so good to me during the summer when I needed somebody, when I thought you'd never forgive me or love me again."

He raised his head and slid his fingers under her chin, gently lifting it so that they were gazing directly at each other.

"I'm never going to hurt you like that again," he vowed. "That is, if you're willing to take a chance on me again."

"Yes, oh, yes!" she cried, barely believing his

198

words. "But this time, with no secrets." She waited anxiously for Jed's response.

Slowly he smiled, then lowered his arms around her waist. For a long moment they stood in a gentle embrace. Then Jed pressed his lips to hers, and they kissed.

Caitlin had her answer and knew that from that moment on nothing in her life would ever be the same.

FRANCINE PASCAL

In addition to collaborating on the Broadway musical *George M!* and the nonfiction book *The Strange Case of Patty Hearst*, Francine Pascal has written several young adult novels, including *Hangin' Out with Cici, My First Love and Other Disasters*, and *Love and Betrayal and Hold the Mayo*. She is also the creator of the Sweet Valley High series. Ms. Pascal has three daughters, Jamie, Susan, and Laurie, and lives in New York City.

JOANNA CAMPBELL

As a teenager in Connecticut, Joanna Campbell was an enthusiastic reader who especially loved books about horses. An accomplished horsewoman herself, Ms. Campbell also sings and plays the piano professionally. She lives in a seacoast town in Maine where she owns an antique store and writes young adult novels (many of which feature her old love, horses!).

Series

Don't miss any of the Caitlin trilogies
Created by Francine Pascal

There has never been a heroine quite like the raven-haired, unforgettable beauty, Caitlin. Dazzling, charming, rich, and very, very clever Caitlin Ryan seems to have everything. Everything, that is, but the promise of lasting love. The three trilogies follow Caitlin from her family life at Ryan Acres, to Highgate Academy, the exclusive boarding school in the posh horse country of Virginia, through college, and on to a glamorous career in journalism in New York City.

Don't miss Caitlin!

THE LOVE TRILOGY

☐	24716-6	**LOVING #1**	$3.50
☐	25130-9	**LOVE LOST #2**	$3.50
☐	25295-X	**TRUE LOVE #3**	$3.50